Twelve NIGHTS

ANDREW ZURCHER

PHILOMEL

PHILOMEL BOOKS

An imprint of Penguin Random House LLC, New York

First published in the United States of America by Philomel,
an imprint of Penguin Random House LLC, 2020.

First published in Great Britain by Puffin UK in 2018.

Visit us online at penguinrandomhouse.com

Library of Congress Cataloging-in-Publication Data is available.

Printed in the United States of America

ISBN 9781524741617

1 3 5 7 9 10 8 6 4 2

Design by Ellice M. Lee.

Text set in Horley Old Style MT.

For my children

Aoife, Una, and Eamon

1

REMOVALS

The sun set at six minutes to four. Kay lay stretched out on the floor, reading the very small print on the back of the newspaper. Her right eye she had squeezed firmly shut; her left was growing deliriously tired, and the tiny words loomed at her amid the blur of her big sinking lashes. More and more she had to close them both, and relax her stiff cheek. More and more she squinted sidelong up at the world, with her head cocked to the right. But if her game caused her irritation, she also felt a sense of modest triumph: she had resisted the temptation to look straight at life since the moment she woke up that morning—exactly eight hours before, according to her watch. Had anyone asked her why she was still keeping her right eye shut at thirteen minutes past four in the afternoon of Christmas Eve, when her mother was going frantic and her little sister, Eloise, was playing jacks by herself in the back room, she wouldn't have known what to say. Keeping her right eye closed was simply something she had to do today, and she was doing it.

Just opposite her head, against the wall, leaned a large metal-framed mirror. Her father had promised to hang it above the hearth, but three months later it still stood there, neglected and collecting dust. Kay regarded herself with curiosity in its dull glass. At school the teachers seemed to talk endlessly about character: having it, getting it, showing it and, above all, building it. Kay was sure she had none, or at least none that was visible. She was the person no one ever really noticed.

A heavy clump of brown hair lay across the corner of her blank brow. She drew it back, straightening it and tucking its length again behind her ear. It didn't make a difference. She searched her own face, letting her gaze linger on her smooth cheek, the simple, mottled bottle-green of her eyes, her flat, pink lips, wondering what others saw when they looked at her. What they didn't see.

No tears.

Her father was still at work—late, as he had been every day

this week and every weekend this month. As he had been every month this year: down at the lab or his office, away for a fortnight on a dig, disappearing off to libraries or meetings—she couldn't keep track. This morning Kay's mum had wiped the counters forcefully after breakfast, then promised her girls a bike ride and a trip to the cinema. But when the sun went down hours later, their winter shoes and coats still lay undisturbed by the door—exactly where they had left them the evening before. Kay could hear the telephone ringing, and she knew it would be her father calling. She could hear the empty distance in his voice as he reported his apologies. Distant, detached, blank.

Just as she was beginning to doze off, her head softly crackling on the open newspaper, her mother burst into the front room, her heels stomping like slippered hammers on the wooden boards. "Get your coat on, Kay, we're going out. Get your sister's coat on."

Five minutes later, as they sat in the back of the car blowing steam in the freezing air and giggling nervously, the two girls still had no idea where they were going, or why. As the engine turned over from gear to gear, in rhythm with the car's regular surges, their nervousness began to subside. Kay's hand still held the warm ache where her sister had been squeezing it. She put it in her lap. The night outside the window seemed sharp and clear, and the mostly white lights in the houses they passed shone with a direct intensity. Her window, by contrast, kept fogging up with her breathing. She moved her face around the glass as far as she could reach, but it was no use. As the car jolted through some lights and then curved down the hill, Ell fidgeted with her foot.

Their mother barked from the front seat, "Eloise, stop it. We'll be out of the car in two minutes."

"But I have something in my boot. It's uncomfortable."

Kay turned to the window again. She counted the streetlamps as they passed, numbering them by their glows on the silvery ground, still frosty from the night before. Her left eye was now growing ridiculously tired—or maybe it was the funny flatness of seeing with just one eye—because in the center of the circle of light cast by every lamp she was sure she could make out a little circular shadow on the ground. Maybe it was just the wisps of foggy breath still clinging to the glass. She was tempted to open her other eye to check—but then, she thought, if she did, and the little dark circles were gone, would that prove that they weren't there, or that they were? Sometimes when you looked right at a star, you couldn't see it; but if you squinted or looked away, you could. And stars were there. Otherwise how would you wish on them?

And then, all at once, she knew where they were going, and why her mother hadn't answered her questions. The car pulled up and stopped outside the familiar gate. Kay went rigid in her seat, feeling her spine arch cold against the comfortable scoop of the fabric behind her. For her part, Ell was obviously disappointed. "I don't want to go to Dad's work," she whined, and kicked her grumpy and uncomfortable boot for emphasis against the seat in front of her.

A night porter sat on duty behind the window at the gate: an old, solid man, stiff and knotted as a fardel of wood, with a curve to his thick back and a white handlebar mustache hanging over a square-set jaw. Kay had never seen him before, but as he shuffled to his feet she recognized the white shirt, black trousers and waistcoat as the uniform of the university's porters. The gate opened, and he waved them through into the parking lot, but then hobbled out of his dimly lit room, down the steps and after the car. He seemed to guess where they would park, because Kay saw him making directly for the spot as her mother doubled round a set of spaces and then reversed back in. He moved with a deliberate and stilted pace, but he still got there just as they were opening the doors.

"Can I help you?" he said to Kay's mum. It was a soft voice

he had, not the sort of rough bark common to university porters. It sounded the way a flannel felt—dense, light and warm—and to Kay it was like a kind extended hand. Yet he stood with his hands dug in his pockets, his fingers working slowly within the fabric, as if turning over coins.

Kay's mum was pulling Ell off the booster seat, then checking the little purple boot absentmindedly. Ell was too old for a child seat now, and far too tall, but she wouldn't stop using it. She couldn't bear to let the small stuff go, couldn't bear for things to change. Her eighth birthday had been a night of tears, and afterward, Kay and her mother had gone from room to room—and even to the car—carefully restoring old and familiar things.

Her mother shook the little boot; a single jack clattered to the ground, which she retrieved and placed in Ell's outstretched hand. "No, thank you," she said. "I'm just here to collect my husband. He's working late."

"Everyone's gone home, I'm afraid, Mrs. . . ." The man trailed off, and Kay watched him arch his bushy left eyebrow, expecting her mother to identify herself.

"Clare. Clare Worth."

The porter looked confused.

That's because she doesn't have Dad's last name, Kay thought. *She's not Mrs. anybody.*

"Well, Mrs. Worth, I'm not telling stories. As I said, I'm afraid everyone has gone home. The only cars still here are mine and old Professor Jackson's that died Tuesday last, God rest him. I've been round the halls to lock up, and the place is sealed proper and shut down tight, lights off and not even a mouse."

Kay felt her mother's arm tense where she was touching it lightly with the palm of her left hand. "I'm sure you're right," she said, "but he did come down to work earlier, so I'll go up and have a look all the same."

"What did you say your husband's name was? Worth?" The old porter sounded soft but insistent, like a wood pigeon maybe. He shuffled his stiff legs quickly to keep his balance. Kay thought for a second that he was almost smiling at the top left corner of his mouth, but then she changed her mind. Or maybe he changed his face.

"More. Dr. More. Edward, I mean. More. He's a fellow at St. Nicholas. He's working on the Fragments Project."

"Well, I can't say as I know the names of the projects," said the old man. "They come and go. But I got a pretty good head for the people, and I don't think I recollect seeing a Dr. More before." He drew a short breath, held his hands up to his face and blew hard on the tips of his fingers, trying to warm them. "But I'm just the night porter around here."

"Oh, you'll definitely have seen him," Kay's mum said. "He's down here almost every evening. Every night."

The porter told her he had a directory and a telephone, and he would save Kay's mum the trouble by calling up to the office. She started to protest, but he had already hobbled painfully round and was walking back to his lodge. Eventually they trailed after him. Kay's mother's hand was cold in hers, but then it would be, in the middle of winter. They waited outside the steps of the tiny lodge—really just a bricked-in nook between two buttresses on the old archeology building, with a lean-to roof and a pretty, circular window. The little window had silver stars stuck in it, and Ell pointed at them and started talking about a card she had made at school with stars just the same, and tinsel. She had repeated herself, twice, to no effect, by the time the porter turned up again in the doorway. Kay felt guilty for having ignored her, and tried to ruffle her hair, but it was drawn back over her scalp as tight as ice.

"I'm afraid I can't find Dr. More on my list," said the porter.

"In fact, I can't find him on the university list either. Edward *M-o-r-e,* you said? Or was that *M-o-o-r-e*? I tried both spellings."

Kay's mum sighed heavily and, leaving the girls, followed the old man back into the hut. They were quiet enough under the window ledge to catch a few snatches of conversation from within. The car park, silent and almost empty, had a few bare trees—saplings of four or five years' growth—dotted at regular intervals down two aisles. Kay remembered that there had been grass here once, but now it was almost all paved. The tree branches glistened black in the bright spotlights from the roofs of the archeology building. The Pitt, they called it. Kay squeezed hard on her left eye, plunging herself into darkness, and gripped Ell's hand more tightly, as if to compensate.

When the door opened, the muted voices suddenly shot out and rebounded around the empty courtyard. Clare Worth was protesting again: ". . . don't understand. I mean, I know you say it's current, but he's definitely here. He's been here for years. I can show you the room."

Kay heard the porter pick up his ring of keys, then pull the door shut behind them as they descended the three or four steps into the car park. Her eyes were still closed, and maybe that was why she heard the crisp echo in the courtyard so acutely, with its single clear report. Each step her mother took made a crack against the frosty stone and pavement.

"What did you say your name was?" Clare was asking the porter as Kay pried open her left eye again.

"Rex. Just Rex," he answered with a wince. He stepped with a stiff hip over a low wall running round the inner grass border of the courtyard, and set off for the near corner where Kay's father had his laboratory and office, on the second floor. Her mother shot him a sharp glance, as if he had just let loose a tarantula, but then—with more resignation—pursued him. She seemed to have forgotten all about her daughters. She didn't speak again, but as she passed by, Kay could see that there were a lot of words in her throat; from the side it looked like it was going to burst open. She and Ell fell back and followed the two adults, holding hands and looking down, watching their feet making tiny depressions in the frost, crunching slightly. Rex had a light step, Kay noticed, because although her mum's new shoes ground visibly into the frozen grass, for all his rough limp and shuffle, Rex's feet didn't seem to make any noise, and hardly any marks at all. All she could hear were his keys jangling on the big ring in his right hand. For a second, in the glare from the spotlights, she saw it very clearly, that ring of keys, and noticed that it had an old-fashioned locking mechanism, with a hinge to open it—like something she had seen at her father's college once, hanging in the manuscript library. Only this ring wasn't plain. She caught another view of it as it swung again briefly into the light. She made out two bits of carving or metalwork, one on the hinge and another on the hasp. She watched for it as they walked, and with glimpse after glimpse, she pieced together the design. It was the same on both sides: a long and sinuous snake entwined with a sword.

He must have been in the army, she decided. *He was probably injured: the limp.*

"His room is on the second floor," her mother was explaining. "And his name is just here on the board—look . . ." And then her voice trailed off, because, as they could all see—and they were all looking—his name was not on the black painted board, the board that was fixed to the wall just outside the door where it had always been, for as long as Kay could remember. The board was there, but not the name—not the name, in its official white lettering, next to the others. Where his name should have been, the board instead said DR. ANDREA LESSING. Her mother pushed through the heavy swinging doors into the stone lobby, and the girls trailed after.

"What's wrong?" Ell whispered to Kay. Her voice was sharp, urgent.

"This is some kind of joke, girls," said Clare Worth, forcing a smile at them. "It's a joke, that's all." She took out her phone and dialed. "I'll try the office again," she was saying. "There was no answer before, but maybe he's back now." They watched her as she listened, as the connection went through. They watched her watching nothing. And then her face went white. "Stay here," she said, her voice suddenly pinched almost to a whisper. Turning, she practically leaped up the stairs.

Kay looked at the ring of keys. She stared at it, at every small detail, one after another, taking them in.

Rex noticed her staring, smiled, unhooked it from his belt and held it out to her. "Have a look if you like," he said with a warm half chuckle. He passed her the whole set. His hands were big and gnarled, like the root ball of an oak. She observed them as she took the keys: oafish but gentle, and somehow slender, too, and as he stretched out his fingers she thought she smelled something sweet, like soft fruit—maybe black currant. But then she had the ring. It held an amazing collection of keys. Even Ell came over to look, which was unusual because she tended to make a point of being officially uninterested in whatever Kay was doing. Kay handled them one by one. The best was an enormous key that looked like a fork with sharp tines, and seemed to be made of gold. It had the same snake and sword cut into it as the ring. And there were three silvery keys, each slightly different from the other, but all with the same kind of shape: a long shaft, with a flat bit fixed at the end—one was square, one circular and one triangular. There were three wooden keys, too—but hard wood, almost like stone, with a gorgeous gold-flecked grain in them. And there were others, short and long, stumpy, heavy. There might have been twenty or thirty of them.

"Stupid keys," said Ell, and she turned toward the full-length mirror that hung against the lobby wall, studying herself. Kay and the porter—Rex—watched her, too. That faint smile was hovering at his cheek again; like Kay, he knew that Ell didn't mean it. Her sister was shorter than Kay by a hand or more. Where Kay was olive-skinned and chestnut-haired, Ell had bright, almost translucent skin, and undulating tresses of a fine, almost golden red. Their father was fond of remarking that their family was composed of four elements. "Your angel mother is the air, as open as the sky. I am the hard and plodding earth," he would say, "but you girls are the quick matter of the world." Kay, he said, was water: silent, deep, cold perhaps, but quick with life. Ell, by contrast, was fire, hot and unpredictable, both creative and destructive.

Moody is more like it, Kay thought. And she smiled, despite herself.

She looked at the grandfatherly porter and thought she should try to be polite. "What are they all for?" she asked.

He was still watching Ell. "Nothing of any consequence now," he answered. "Just look at that beauty," he added, almost as if to himself. "I'll wager she won't need any keys at all."

Taking the steps two at a time, Ell had begun to jump up the spiral staircase in her fur-edged purple rubber boots. They were a little too big, a hand-me-down gift from Kay which she had not yet quite grown into. They made her seem smaller than she was: clumsy, a little delicate. At the fifth or sixth step she turned round, grinning impishly, her face flushed and radiant after the cold air outside, her full lips pink and puckered. With an air of priestlike gravity, as if she were performing a sacred ritual, she took her hand from her pocket, opening her palm to reveal three of the jacks she had been playing with earlier at home. "Knucklebones," their father called them; it was that rare thing, a game he approved of, and he always said the same thing: "a very ancient game of skill—and chance." Ell was the acknowledged master of anything and everything to do with jacks, and she wore her title with pride. Now she tossed the little stars into the air, flipped her slender hand with a dancer's grace and caught them neatly upon her knuckles.

Kay smiled. *Show-off.*

It is sometimes the case that something exceptionally beautiful happens just before a calamity. The calamity even seems to reach back in time and twiddle the beautiful thing round, making it even more beautiful because of what is about to happen—or anyway, Kay thought, that's how it comes to seem.

Ell looked so beautiful standing there, her lips grinning and pursed at once, her eyes dancing in the light from the lantern in the center of the lobby, her radiant red hair now loosely draped across her shoulders, her whole form alight with daring and mischief. And then she started to take another step in those stupid purple boots, and tripped, and fell, and her face hit the floor. The jacks clattered onto the stones before her outstretched hand.

In the gap before she could cry out, the porter, Rex, jumped to his feet and sprang lightly over to her. He reached down, lithe and strong, and caught her up. The movement was sinuous, the spring and cradle entirely balletic. Kay hardly had time to breathe before he was sitting down again, the whole sobbing form of her sister tightly, snugly nestled in his arms. She watched, at once shocked and mesmerized. For her part, Ell settled into Rex's arms as if he were a hearth.

Slowly he rocked her; slowly the little girl's sobs subsided. Kay noticed she was gripping Rex's keys so hard that her hand had turned white; a piece of sharp iron had made a welt on the edge of her palm. She held them out. The noise shook Rex from something like a reverie, and he looked up at her. Everything seemed to be happening very slowly. Ell sat up on his knee, as if awaking, and she, too, looked at Kay. Rex took the keys. Still he stared. And then Kay saw it: a perfect symmetry between the old man and the little girl—as if cut from a single stone by the same hand, as if painted in the same colors, as if sung by the same singer, they regarded her with their heads at an angle, their eyes at one focus, their mouths equally parted. All was equal. Kay froze.

"Sometimes," Rex said slowly, somehow at once both fulfilling and breaking the spell, "something exceptionally beautiful happens just before a calamity."

Every hair on the back of Kay's neck stood up, but not in fear. His eyes were too kind for that—as if they were the eyes of her own sister. Sometime. Somehow. Or something.

"I think these are yours," he said to Ell as he tipped the three spilled jacks from his palm into hers. Ell looked at them, picked one out and presented it back to him. It fell into his open hand, a gift.

Just then Clare Worth came running two at a time down the spiral stairs. She sprinted past them, out through the double doors and into the courtyard. Rex set Ell on her feet, then, with some deliberateness, put his hands on his knees, pushing himself up. Slipping the jack in his pocket and hooking the keys back onto his belt, he held the girls' hands, and they walked after Clare Worth as quickly as they could. A few minutes later, safely belted in the back seat of the car, both girls turned as their mother—oblivious—pulled out of the Pitt car park and away from their father's office. They were still stunned, watching for the old man on his step. He stood there, looking, Kay thought, like a man composed all of sadness, like someone condemned for a crime he did not commit. His hand was raised in farewell.

It was the same at St. Nick's. No one seemed to know

Edward More there, either; and the college room where Kay had spent her half-term holidays, looking impatiently out of the window at the afternoon activity, had someone else's name over the door. In fact, it had the same name over the door as that on the board in the Pitt: DR. ANDREA LESSING. Only this time the light inside was on, and the woman who answered Clare Worth's knocking appeared to be as surprised as they were. She was tall, but also somehow small and delicate, and Kay thought her bones were probably as thin and wispy as her gold hair. She was wrapped up in serpentine coils of scarves and throws.

"I have no idea what you can possibly mean," she said. "I've had these rooms for the last fifteen years. I've never had any other rooms for as long as I have been at St. Nick's. Have a look round," she continued, stepping back from the door and gesturing around the room with fine, elegant fingers. Kay thought they looked, each one, like nimble snakes, writhing with venom and muscle. "These are my books, my things, my work." Kay's mum had been frantically explaining while two porters hovered nervously on the stairs behind them, unsure whether to intervene. "I really can't help you," Dr. Andrea Lessing added. "In fact, I was just about to go home for the holiday." She started to close the door, but Clare Worth had seen something, and she wedged her foot firmly in the way.

"I don't know you," she said accusingly. Kay shrank from the menace in her mother's voice.

"I am sorry for that, but I hardly think it's my fault," replied Dr. Andrea Lessing.

"Are you an archeologist?" Clare Worth's eyes moved more wildly now, ranging around the room, trying to make out the titles of the books just to the left of the door. The light was low. Kay noticed that her own leg was shaking, so she pressed her foot hard into the floor of the staircase. "I see you have some of the same books my husband has," she said. "*Many* of the same books, in fact. Do you work on the Fragments Project?"

"Mrs. More—"

"My name is Worth."

"Mrs. Worth, really, I'm sorry, I don't have time for this. Yes, I do work on the Fragments Project, but no, I really must ask you to let me close the door and get home to my family." Dr. Andrea Lessing was pushing the door closed. Kay's mum's foot was sliding back on the wooden boards. Then her heel hit the ridge where the raised lip of the door frame blocked the draft. Her foot held. There was an awkward silence, and the porters started to shift, leaning forward as if about to intervene. Kay drew a breath and raised her hand to reach out, to touch her mother on the shoulder or at the vulnerable place at the tip of her elbow. She wanted to get her out of this place. Instead, Ell's hand shot out and took hers; her face was fierce and full.

"Do you know about the Bride of Bithynia?" It was her mother's most level, grave, but also, now, desperate tone.

Kay knew it the way she knew how the stone outcrop behind her house felt to her knee when she smashed down upon it with her full weight. She knew it as well as she knew the tread of the stairs to her room, the soft click of the door's latch behind her and the comforting, lofty quiet of her top bunk—she knew that the diminutive Dr. Andrea Lessing had to be pushing with enormous force, because this door suddenly slammed shut on her mother, knocking her back onto her left foot and very nearly crushing Kay and Ell against the cold and flaking plaster of the stairwell.

As they stumbled out of the staircase and back into the college's open courts, Clare Worth looked dazed, her daughters not less so. The porters were clearly distressed and apologetic. For some reason they could not explain or understand, they felt a sympathy for Clare Worth, whom they knew they knew, though they couldn't say the first thing about Edward More. They kept saying so, in muted tones one to one another, as they walked back through Sealing Court. Clare Worth seemed to have given up trying to understand. The porters held the door for the girls as they stepped through the wicket of the Tree Court gate, back into Litter Lane, where they had distractedly ditched the car half an hour before. With gingerly moving fingers, the two men ushered the gate closed behind them, as softly as they could, trying not to give the impression, Kay thought, that they were shutting them out. But they *were.* And the moment the lock clicked, Kay's mum began to cry. She didn't move from the gate or put her hands to her face. She just looked down. The only sound Kay could hear was a ventilation fan up the alley, pumping out steam and the smell of grease from the college kitchens. Ell shivered at Kay's light touch.

"Mum," Kay said.

"Yes, Katharine, what?"

"Mum, there was something strange about that porter at the Pitt. Rex."

"What, Katharine?" She was still crying. Clare Worth

didn't sob when she cried, but the tears now came quickly and heavily.

"Well, for one thing, when you were walking up to Dad's office—well, what *should* have been Dad's office—and the courtyard was really quiet, your feet were making a lot of noise on the stone, and you were leaving footprints in the grass. And so were we. I checked." Ell had been kicking a cobble. Now she stopped.

"Yes, of course, Kay." Clare was reaching in her pocket to find an old tissue, which she laboriously picked apart and flattened. She sounded annoyed. Kay took and squeezed Ell's hand while she waited, but Ell pulled it away and stared hard at her sister, as if to warn her off, to make her stop. Ell was always telling her not to bother Mum, not to stick her nose into other people's business.

"Well, you know how that old porter had a limp or something? And he walked heavily? But he didn't leave any prints on the grass, and I don't think I could hear his feet on the cobbles at all."

"Katharine." Clare Worth exchanged the tissue in her hand for the keys in her pocket and unlocked the car. "That's the very least of my worries right now. Something horrible is going on, and footprints in the frost don't matter. Not at all."

She stood up and bore down on her daughters with newly hardened eyes. "Now get in."

In the back of the car, Ell's face was wearing that fierce look again. *Told you,* said her eyes.

So Kay didn't mention the other things on her mind: Ell's fall, the strange kindness and familiarity of the porter, and something she thought she'd seen in the room at St. Nick's—what should have been her father's room, but was the room of Dr. Andrea Lessing. Something she had seen while her mother was being pushed back onto her left foot as the door closed abruptly behind the enormous strength of a very slight woman. Instead the two girls sat quietly and the car moved slowly, almost reluctantly, through the empty, dark streets, past the reaching winter spines of the chestnuts and the hawthorns and the oaks and the beeches and, above all, the countless lime trees, blacker than the visible light of the black night. And she didn't ask about the Bride of Bithynia, and they ate their cold supper where it still sat on the plates Clare Worth had set out in the afternoon. And because of the tears that sometimes drew and dropped down their mother's cheeks, the girls did as they were asked, or expected, and never once thought of their baubled and tinseled tree, unlit, or of the wooden box that contained their stockings, which in the past they had always hung from the mantel on Christmas Eve. And they never once dared open the door of their father's study, for fear of the emptiness Kay was sure would lie within it—the vacant shelves, the cleared desk, the stacks of papers that would not stand there on the floor where they had always stood before. The girls never once uttered a single word. Instead they brushed their teeth, and they dressed for bed, and they turned off the light. And all the time, without speaking at all, Kay kept her right eye shut, and Ell picked at her hands, and Clare Worth wiped those occasional tears from the bottom of her jaw on the left side, so that they didn't drip on her blouse.

But when Kay climbed up into her bunk bed, she felt something on her pillow. It was a card. She knew at once that she hadn't left a card on her bed. It was small and stiff, about the size of the train tickets they sometimes got when Mum took them to Ely for a summer picnic. Kay held it up. She couldn't read the writing at first, but a light shone from her mother's room, where—uncharacteristically—she was sobbing a little, and a shaft of it, shooting through a crack in the door, caught the card as Kay turned it. Then the silvery letters leaped out, glittering in her hands. It read:

Will O. de Wisp, *Gent.* F.H.S.W.P.
and
Philip R. T. Gibbet, *Gent.* F.H.S.W.P.

Removals

Kay blinked at the card in the half-light, uncomprehending. She was exhausted, and as usual, Ell had fallen asleep on the bottom bunk the moment her head hit the pillow. Listening to her deep breaths made Kay the drowsier, and she looked more and more vacantly at the strange card as it clung to the light in her weakening hand. Just before her left lid finally collapsed, and just as her hand was dropping out of its shaft of light, she might briefly have glimpsed the other side of the card, with its carefully stenciled and embossed silver emblem—the very symbol that, an hour before, she thought she had seen on a book lying on Dr. Andrea Lessing's wide wooden desk; a symbol she definitely *had* seen several times that day: the body of a snake entwined with the blade of a sword.

"Is it done?"

"Yes."

"And have they left no trace?"

"Nothing."

"And the children?"

"The children?"

"Has no one taken order for the children?"

"But—"

"You are a fool."

"But the order sheet—"

"You are every one of you fools. Did I not use the old words so that you might understand? Did I not speak them in your ear, as in the old tales that you love? The snake must strike with the sword."

"It will be done as you say."

"They must all be destroyed—the thieving fox and his little cubs."

"As you order it, so it will be."

"See that it is."

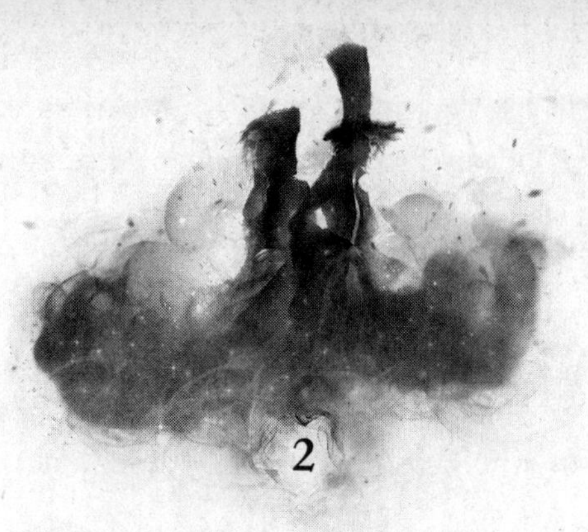

2

THE AUTHOR

Kay was suddenly aware that she had been hearing voices. It was completely dark, so it had still to be night. She turned over very quietly onto her right side, and strained into her ears to hear. At first, still drowsy, she thought it was her mother talking on the phone; but these were low voices, men's voices, and distant—maybe downstairs or in the garden. Then she realized, again at a stroke, that it was only dark because her eyes were closed. Though at first slightly afraid to look, she cracked her left eye open imperceptibly. Everything appeared as black as if she had left it shut—until she saw what seemed to be a flash of light like a headlight sweeping across her window.

But no, she was imagining it. It was nothing but the wind,

the moon. Her father said she had *such* an imagination. *Give her a pebble,* he said, *and she will build a castle.*

"Ow!" It was a whisper, or a kind of sharp and hissing breath, but it was loud and unmistakable.

"It's hardly my fault you're so slow. Or that we're gamboling about on gables for the second time in twelve hours."

"We've been over this already. I couldn't have known she would take it with her. It's not altogether customary to go about town with someone's tooth in your pocket, now, is it? I admit I was wrong last time—"

"You couldn't have been *more* wrong last time—"

"And I said I admit it. But that's quite a different matter. Failing to collect a tooth and omitting—well, omitting a whole body are not, the last time I looked, even on the same page of the code."

"You didn't just miss the body."

Kay was more alert now, and her left eye widened. The voices were coming from outside, and there was a light, a light that every so often swept across her window behind the curtain. *It must be a flashlight,* she thought. There had been a fair amount of grunting and scrabbling, but that stopped now.

"Look, you weren't there. As I testified at the tribunal, it was an honest mistake. The order said, *Archduke Bartolomeo, Prince of Prussia,* and the address was a villa in Vienna. So I went to the place, searched it and identified the subject. I followed procedure and submitted the order sheet. He must have known I was coming. It's not my fault he switched the body—I mean, *his* body—for someone else's. And it looked the same to me; it was right where I'd left it, under a mulberry tree in a courtyard garden, wrapped in a silk kaftan. Still haven't figured out how he knew I was coming."

"That's hardly the point. You removed the emperor, by the muses!"

"Well, that was a bit on the embarrassing side, I admit. But how was I to know he was the emperor? It's not as if I'd ever seen him up close. Emperor Shmemperor. And like I said, he was just where I'd left the archduke, all wrapped up and dozing under the mulberry tree, as dukishly as you like. Arch as can be. Now, what's an emperor doing dozing under a mulberry tree? I ask you."

"He was wearing the imperial crown, Will."

"Look, Flip, I'm in removals now. I'm a removals guy. I'm not a herald, I'm not a lawyer and I'm definitely not an emperor.

For better or worse—mainly, if truth be told, for worse—I'm in removals. I remove."

"By the stones, Will, you may be my best friend, but you're still half idiot. Ow!"

Then the grunting started again, and Kay heard a scraping noise—the tiles, the tiles on the lower part of the roof. She flinched; these voices were close.

"Anyway, this is hardly comparable. We'll just pop in, find the tooth and get out again. Couldn't be simpler."

"When it comes to working with you, Will, nothing is ever simple."

The light outside the curtain was bright now, and Kay reckoned they were just on the other side of the window. Something was sounding a note in her head like the muffled bell of a broken alarm clock. *A tooth?* What were they talking about?

Kay tried to sit up straight, but the blood rushed from her head and the world spun giddily around her. And then she remembered the card that had been on her pillow—the card that was now under her pillow. She pulled it out and looked at it again. There at the bottom, in large letters, it clearly read, ***Removals***. So these were the removers, Will O.

de Wisp and Philip R. T. Gibbet. But who were they here to remove?

Like a wave it broke on her: they were talking about her father's tooth—his wisdom tooth, which he had had removed last year and had given her (reluctantly) because she had asked him for it. She'd begged him for it, in fact. To remember him. *I'm not going anywhere, Kay,* he'd said. Her mother had snorted from the next room. Now she kept the tooth in the left pocket of her cardigan, which was hanging—where?—on the near post of her bed. The cardigan she had been wearing on Christmas Eve. Today. Yesterday.

The voices were very close now, close to the window, probably shoved up against the ledge. All the scrabbling and scraping against the roof tiles, so clear in the dark stillness of the house, had stopped. In the silence she could hear the latch turning. As quickly as she could, she reached out her hand, stretched down until the blood screamed in her head, felt her way into the pocket of her cardigan and retrieved the tooth. She put it in the palm of her right hand, which she clenched into a fist under her pillow. Then she closed her open eye and, pressing her head with great purpose into the soft down, pretended to be asleep.

Every space has its own noise, like a fingerprint. Most of the time no one notices this noise, of course—it might be a hum, or in some seasons an occasional creak, a draft, the skittering of birds or maybe mice or hedgehogs in the garden. In the winter, for the girls' room, this ambient noise was the quiet voice of the tall evergreens two or three meters outside their window, swaying in the wind or scraping against the corner of the house when disturbed by some night-foraging animal. As Kay lay in her bed with her eyes tightly closed (*too tightly?*—she relaxed them) and her right hand clutching her father's tooth beneath her pillow, that familiar noise changed completely—opened up as a draft swept in past the curtain.

Kay's heart stamped.

"Ow!" One of them tripped off the sill, crashed through the curtain and landed heavily on the floor. Kay held her breath, certain that her mother would have heard it, or that Ell at least would wake up.

"Sshhh," said a voice from the window. And then, "Is this tooth really necessary? What happens if we just leave it?"

"Flip, if you want to go back and submit the order sheet to Ghast without all the movables accounted for, that's up to you." Will sounded like he was sitting up as he whispered, "To be perfectly frank with you, after the whole Habsburg business, I don't mind if I never see Ghast's dirty little nostrils widen at me again . . . Hmm. I think I may develop a bruise."

"Well, I hope so," said Flip. "There'd be no fun left in pushing you if you didn't get hurt once in a while."

At this Kay dared to crack her left eye open again. Between the fuzz of her parting lashes she saw the light of the flashlight held in the hand emerging from behind the curtain. It was pointing at the wall opposite her—or, rather, panning the wall as Flip began searching for the tooth.

"Where do you reckon she keeps it?" Flip said, the top of his head curling round the heavy curtain to look down at Will, who was still rubbing his shin.

In the dim light Kay could see almost nothing about them, except that they both seemed very tall, almost stretched or elongated—like the thinned and distorted shadows of normal shapes cast by a light lying on the ground.

"And would you mind getting up to help me, please?" said Flip as an impossibly endless leg (*like a spider's,* Kay thought) came swinging over the sill and under the curtain. The rest of him followed lankily into the cramped room. Flip turned immediately back to the far wall—to the bookcase, the chest of drawers and the small pile of toys still tumbled in the corner where Ell had left them that morning. Which was lucky, because what Will said next made Kay, for only the tiniest second, open her eye very wide indeed—and had Flip been looking in her direction, he could not have missed it.

"The order sheet," said Will noisily as he unfolded a crumpled piece of paper retrieved from his coat, "says it will be in the left pocket of her cardigan. Or, with a very low probability, in her right hand."

"Cardigan?" asked Flip.

"Bedpost," Will shot back. And then the light swung round, and Flip's body followed it, leaving Kay a split second to squeeze her eye shut again. She held her breath and concentrated on not moving her right fist, with its now precious prize, even an inch. But for all her heroic self-control, for all her theatrical stillness, she knew it was already too late. Over the top of his paper, even as he spoke, Will's eyes had settled directly upon her.

Kay felt everything change around her.

Everything.

"Flip," breathed Will, staring at Kay in a way that she

could feel all over her face, despite the fact that her eyes were jammed shut. "Flip, we have a problem."

Kay's heart hammered a path right out of her chest and into her throat. It was suddenly so tight in her head that she could hardly hear them as they carried on talking.

"Will, you *are* a problem," answered Flip. "What now?"

For an instant there was complete silence, and Kay was dimly aware of the sound of the fir tree outside scraping against the gutter.

"We've been witnessed," Will said in the same low and measured voice. "It's all right, little girl, you can open your eye," he said. "We won't bite."

"But I read the order sheet. The order sheet doesn't say anything about her being a witness." Flip was whispering hard, like a hawk plummeting to strike, as he stepped over to Will and took the papers. He hauled Will to his feet and then began to scan them. "Nope," he said, running his finger down the page. "No, no, no, no. No powers, no history, no prophecy, no witness. She's entirely clean. No bio on her whatsoever. She can't see us. She can't see us for what we really are."

"She can see us all right," said Will, peering at Kay. He was so tall that his head, slightly bowed under the pitch of the sloping ceiling, was level with her own as she lay on the top bunk. He cocked it to one side to look straight at her. "Hello," he said in a friendly voice, cracking a smile. "Hello, little witness. Let's have a look at you."

Kay lay huddled back against the wall as his gathering hands suddenly loomed out of the darkness toward her, but it was no use resisting—he was as strong as he was tall, and despite the wadded blankets he had her sitting up in a second. She buried her right hand behind her, almost sitting on it under a lump of duvet.

"Ah. I think we've located the tooth," Will said over his shoulder. "In her hand, just as the sheet says."

Kay had a good, one-eyed stare at him in the indirect light from the flashlight, which Flip had trained on the pages of the order sheet as he raced hurriedly through them. Will was broad and tall but, on more careful consideration, strangely skinny. The light almost seemed to shine through his shoulders. His neck also appeared normal enough until you looked right at it, when it would suddenly seem to stretch, or twist, or narrow—or something. She couldn't put her finger on it. He was dressed in a long robe or cloak like a housecoat, with a thick rope belt around his waist. The cuffs of his sleeves flared like trumpets, but his wrists were as bony and slender as everything else about him, seeming to disappear into the cavity of his clothing. *Like the tongue of a flame in a sooty lamp, like a wraith from the darkness conjuring.* But he had been so strong, she thought, lifting her up and setting her back on the bed as if she were almost weightless. And, she noticed suddenly as she searched again for his face, he had a strange way of looking at you with only one of his eyes at a time, or perhaps with both eyes but differently. And with his left eye he was now studying her very closely. He leaned forward, putting his chin on the edge of her mattress, his elegantly fingered hands tucked up beneath it.

"So," he said in a very soft and winning voice, "are you going to give us the tooth? Because I for one would like to go home and get some rest."

Kay shook her head slowly, then a bit faster.

Will's smile dissipated. He frowned comically at her from beneath furrowed brows. "You're not?" he asked. He stuck out his lower lip.

Kay shook her head again.

"She says she's not going to give us the tooth," said Will over his shoulder.

Flip was still running his finger down page after page of

the order sheet, and seemed not to be able to hear anything but his own murmuring.

Will turned back to the bed. "Why? Don't you want me to get some rest?" He tried smiling again.

Kay stared at him. She wasn't sure she could speak even if she wanted to. Her throat felt as if it had suddenly been transformed into a brown paper bag.

"It's just that that tooth is extremely important to my career prospects," Will said, nodding. "If I don't bring it back to my boss, I might get, you know, laid off." He shook his head. "And then what would I do? Freelance fabling? Not a good line of work," he went on, pausing with two very angular, narrow eyebrows raised. "Ethically very dubious."

"Will." Flip looked up from his papers with a desperate blankness. "They're not all here. The papers. The order sheet. There's another page. Look—here, at the bottom . . . it says, *page eighteen of nineteen*, and then that's it, that's the last sheet. So there's another one. Where is the last sheet, Will? Will, tell me you have the last sheet." Flip had moved quickly over to the bed, and in a frenzied haste was digging his hands into Will's cloak pockets.

Will, who had stood up slightly stiffly with a sort of doomed but resigned look on a face that now looked lined and haggard, was shoving his own hands deep into other pockets. Kay could hear the chink of metal and the rustle of paper, and many other strange noises besides as the four hands groped around inside more pockets than she could keep track of, pockets that seemed to dive well beyond the depth of a standard lining.

Flip was in up to his elbows when Will suddenly brightened. "Here, I think I've got it."

It was a piece of paper folded up very bulkily into a small square. In the dim light Will began gingerly to unpick it from its various tucks and creases.

"Oh, yes, I remember now," he said as he undid the last fold and tried to flatten it out against the side of Kay's bed, gently stretching along the creases. "I had a terrible sneezing fit just as Ghast gave me the order, and—"

"I'll have that," Flip broke in as he swiped the paper impatiently from Will's hand and began to read.

Will made a face at Kay that seemed to say, *Yuck*. She almost giggled.

"Oh no. No—for the love of all that follows, no. Will, you really are a walking catastrophe."

With a quick snatch of her left hand, Kay grabbed the

corner of her duvet and drew it up over her knees and around her shoulders. The air in the room had become uncomfortably cold, and the curtain continued to flutter with the light breeze outside. She huddled in the top corner of her bed and flexed her right fist behind her, feeling the edges of her father's tooth in her palm. That hand was clammily hot; the rest of her body, by contrast, was freezing. The cold would be sure to wake Ell, she thought, for Ell was a light sleeper at the best of times. Wasn't she? *Eloise, how are you sleeping through this?*

Oh, Eloise, please don't wake up.

Will had gone back to watching Kay intently—or, rather, watching intently that part of her right arm that disappeared behind her back—while Flip kept up his agitated reading and muttering.

"You're not going to believe this," Flip said with a sigh, looking up. Kay saw the same angular face, the same high brows, the same strange gaze. "I'd better read it to you in full."

"If it means Ghast is going to dazzle me with his nasal musculature, I'd really rather you didn't." Will laid his right cheek gently on the mattress and closed his left eye. Kay noticed how, although his brows were black, his hair shone a silvery white in the low light from Flip's flashlight.

"No, I'm afraid you have to hear this. It's an order proviso, double underlined, at the foot of the inventory. It's in Ghast's own hand. *Note,* it says. *Domestic removal must be performed while the subject's family is off the premises. Under no circumstances attempt to capture subject or movables in their presence. Do not approach them, even in their sleep.* Did you hear that, Will? We're not even supposed to be here. Oh, for the love of the nine sisters, I can't believe this." He paused and took a deep breath. "But there's more. This is the best bit. You're going to love this," he said, looking up with an expression that seemed to suggest anything but love, and stared at Will's hunched back. "*Subject's daughter is an author.* She's not a witness, you unplottable oaf, she's an *author.*"

Only then, when he stopped speaking, did Kay realize that Will had begun quietly humming to himself—a quick, zippy sort of song. But he stopped at those last words, and there was total silence in the room. Not even the garden's evergreen boughs stirred in this void.

"An *author,*" Flip repeated quietly, and his arm fell to his side, and the flashlight drooped until its beam shone directly, and very brightly, on the tiny patch of carpet in front of his left knee. Kay was relieved to find herself back in the anonymity of near darkness. Her heart had stopped racing now, and the violent trembling that had made her gather up her duvet had subsided. She thought, as she suddenly found herself swallowing easily and clearing the lump in her throat, that she could speak. So she did.

"Excuse me," she said. And, more timidly, "Who are you?"

Will propped his chin back up on the mattress and opened his eye, staring directly into her face from the gloom. His iris looked a deep and inexhaustible gray, and in this light the crow's feet opening into his cheeks seemed to gape like cracks.

Those cracks. Kay was scared she might fall into one of them. "And what do you mean, I'm an author, please?"

"We're going to have to tell her everything," Will said to Flip as he continued to regard her carefully but kindly. And then, after a pause, very softly, he said, "An author. I never thought I would see another author."

Flip, who had been kneeling bowed on the floor, stood up slowly, as if he were extraordinarily tired. He lifted the flashlight, throwing the beam again around the room; Kay watched him carefully as he turned and, though still slightly stooped, lifted his shoulders to their full height. He passed the light to his right hand, came up beside Will, put his left arm over his shoulder and then lifted the flashlight up onto the top bunk, resting it on the bottom corner of the duvet, pointing toward the back wall.

"I'm Flip," he said, "and this is Will. We're wraiths."

Kay stared at them, then tried swallowing again.

From the darkness conjuring.

"I knew that much," she said. They both started. "Your names, I mean. It's because I woke up when you were coming up the roof. I heard what you were saying," she explained. "But I don't understand what you're doing here, or why you left me this card, or why you want my father's tooth. Or anything. And I wish you would close the window before Ell and I catch cold." With her left hand, she handed Will the card as Flip ducked behind him to pull the window shut.

"Flip, we should do this introduction properly," Will said. Flip nodded slowly with his lips pursed pensively together. "It's like this," Will went on. "I'm Will O. de Wisp, wraith and removals man, Fellow of the Honorable Society of Wraiths and Phantasms." He stepped back and bowed. "This is my friend Flip Gibbet, also of the Honorable Society and, well, also in removals. We've got an order here from the Sergeant of the Honorable Society to remove your father; an order that comes directly from the top. We started the job this morning and finished with the movables this evening, but we neglected to collect one item—the tooth I think you are hiding in your fist back there—so we had to come back before we could submit for completion. This card"—he tapped its edge with his impossibly slender finger, temporarily at a loss for words—"it's a little pleasure of mine, to leave a trace. Normally we wouldn't have had any trouble with it—normally no one can see us, not properly. Normally no one can make much sense of the card, if they notice it in the first place. Normally. But seeing as you're an author . . ." He stumbled over this again, and for a moment breathed quickly. "As you're an author," he repeated, "you overheard us and woke up and got involved, and, well, now we have to deal with you."

Kay looked at Flip, who was nodding slightly, his head tilted to his shoulder. Suddenly he seemed to have thought of or remembered something, and he reached quickly into one of his cloak pockets.

"I'm sure I've got one somewhere," he said. And then he pulled out a black eyepatch like a pirate's, and held it out to her.

"You might be needing this for a short while, just till your eyes get used to it. It could be easier on the cheeks."

Leaning forward slightly, Kay took it carefully from him, only to draw quickly back again to pin her right arm against the wall. Settled, she looked at the patch in her hand, where it lay like a dark blot in the darker darkness.

"Will," said Flip. "Something tells me this one isn't going to need a patch."

Will hadn't shifted or broken Kay's gaze, but suddenly he seemed to be staring into her eyes as if she were the dawn and he had waited all night to see her rise.

"Yes," he said. "Yes. Keep the patch if you like, but for now, try opening your eyes. Just"—and here he folded his arms up and across his chest, then spread them out like a flower blooming, to take in the whole of the dark room around them—"just try to keep looking at the world *lightly*. Or don't try—just let it happen. See with two eyes as if they were one."

Kay thought maybe the wraiths might try to steal the tooth while her eyes were shut, that it was all a ruse. For a second she tensed. But the lightness in her face was too great a pleasure to be surrendered. She let her lids fall gently closed, relaxing all the muscles in her face. It was such a relief that it almost hurt. *Lightly*. She opened her eyes.

The wraiths were still there. Kay's lids blinked fast as a butterfly.

"Now you're practically one of us," said Will. And then, his face changing, he added hurriedly, "Ma'am."

Kay stared stupidly back at them, not sure what to say. Her mother was always telling her to be frank, and never to use two words where she could make herself understood with one. She cut to the chase.

"What do you mean, you have to deal with me? Why do you want the tooth? Where have you put my father?"

Flip answered this time. "Well—ma'am," he said, looking quickly (and was it questioningly?) at Will, "it's as my colleague says. We had an order to remove your father, and we did; and when you remove someone, you also have to take all the movables, the things associated with that person, so that no trace of them survives in the place from which they have been removed. And we have a complete inventory of his movables"—here he held up the first eighteen pages of the order sheet he had studied so carefully—"but my *esteemed* partner here"—and here he turned pointedly, at very close range, to Will, and clownishly stuck out the tip of his tongue—"managed to miss one item, the tooth, during completion this afternoon. So here we are."

They were clearly not used to explaining themselves, Kay thought. She noticed that she had relaxed her grip a bit on the duvet, and she shifted her weight slightly to make herself more comfortable. She sat up a bit higher.

"It's not every day," Flip went on, "that a wraith runs into a witness while on a job, but when it happens, well, you have to remove the witness, too. Then the Sergeant settles it."

Kay looked at them, a bit more nervously now. She still had no idea what was involved in being "removed" or what an "author" was, and she was about to ask when Flip suddenly prevented her by adding quickly, "But of course we can't remove *you*, you being an author and all." He smiled brightly and looked at Will.

Will looked puzzled. "We can't?" he said.

"No, we can't," said Flip with finality.

Kay broke in abruptly. "But what is—"

Just then, more abruptly still, from the bunk below, Ell gave a loud yawn, murmured something only partly intelligible and turned heavily over in her sleep. They had all forgotten her. After a moment of what looked like panic in the two wraiths' faces, only Kay was left in a slight agitation, anxious lest Ell should wake up and get removed herself.

Flip, cool again, seemed to understand her worry before she voiced it. "It's quite all right. According to the order sheet, which is always correct, neither your mother nor your sister can see us or hear us—I mean, *really* see us for what we are. Had they received our calling card, they wouldn't have noticed it. They'd have thought it a blank scrap. Had they heard our voices, it would have been the wind moaning. If they'd bumped into us, they would have persuaded themselves that we were other people entirely, or perhaps that they had imagined us. It's a trick in the way you look at things, or the way you get others to look at things." With one long, elegant finger, he tapped his temple at the corner of his eye. "Only witnesses can really see us."

"And authors, obviously," Will added.

"So there's really no chance she'll wake up," Flip concluded. For the first time since he had clambered through her window, Kay thought he sounded perfectly relaxed.

"Who are you?" Ell asked sleepily from the bunk below.

Now, Kay thought, the wraiths really were stunned. They stood so rigid that they bumped their heads on the ceiling.

"Was this on the order sheet?" Will asked.

Flip shook his head. Very slowly, they let their eyes sink to the lower bunk, then inclined their heads and dipped their shoulders; and soon they were both doubled over, staring intensely at Ell. She was rubbing her right eye with her right fist. Her strawberry curls bobbed softly about her round, plump face as she herself bobbed slightly, still waking from a deep sleep. She yawned again, and propped herself up a bit higher on her elbow.

"Are you visiting Mum?" she asked, looking back and forth from one to the other. "Is Dad back? Is Kay here?"

Kay was here; in fact, she was already on the bunk ladder, and it wasn't two seconds before she was beside her little sister, her right hand and the tooth already firmly dug in behind them in a wad of duvet, as before.

"This," said Flip, "is unexpected in the very extremest sense."

"This is downright creepy," agreed Will.

"If we go with you," Kay said quickly, "can we get our father back?"

Flip had already started to shake his head, and was about to explain about the irreversibility of removal, when Will cut him off abruptly.

"That's something you'd have to take up with Sergeant Ghast," he said. "But I'm sure he would be only too happy to discuss it with you. And we could have you there very quickly."

Flip began to protest. "Will, she's a child, and it's a day's flight, and Ghast—"

"No, Flip. In all our years, we've never left an author behind—and this one is something special, or I'm not a phantasm."

"What's a phantasm," Kay blurted. It wasn't even a question, but Will seemed to prefer her interjections to Flip's.

"A wraith," Will said. Kay blinked. "An appearance. Something or someone that appears. Someone who is both there and not there."

"So you're not really here?"

"I'm here," Will answered.

"I'm not," said Flip with an exasperated shake of his head. "I'm off." He strode to the window and levered his long body between the curtains. They heard him slide across the short slope of the roof, then swing down to the ground. His footsteps crunched away across the frosty grass.

Will stepped to the window and drew back the curtain. The night beyond was black and moonless. He looked back at the girls. The expression on his face was unreadable, lost between excitement and concern, impatience and unwillingness. If he'd had a thousand minds, Kay thought, he'd have been in all of them.

"Fine," said Kay decisively, "we'll go. But I keep the tooth."

"What tooth? Go where?" asked Ell. "Where are we going, Kay?"

"To find Dad," she replied. Just then the window, off its latch, swung in a gust wildly against the metal frame, then back out into the wide, black, icy night.

“Bring him before me.”

“As you order it.”

“Let him not speak. We shall hear no tales tonight. Tighten the bridle.”

“It is done.”

“See, all of you, what it is to give up your life to fond hopes and foolish dreams. Look how time hangs on him like a ragged cloth. The dirt of it crusts on his skin. And when you cut him—watch, all of you; watch how he bleeds. There is nothing so frail as blood, nothing so delicate. It rises and it falls. Its passions are unpredictable. It deceives the mind with visions. It binds the heart to its wild fantasies. Blood is a weakness.”

“But the wound—”

“It is not mortal. Truss him, you two, and take him to the Imaginary. It will amuse me to think of him lying there, feeble and all but forgotten. If I think of him.”

“As you order it.”

“Let it be an instruction to you.”

“It will be.”

"A moment. Remind me. By what name do our enemies call him?"

"They call him the Builder."

"So they do. The Builder. Let him build in the Imaginary what castles he can. Bind him tightly."

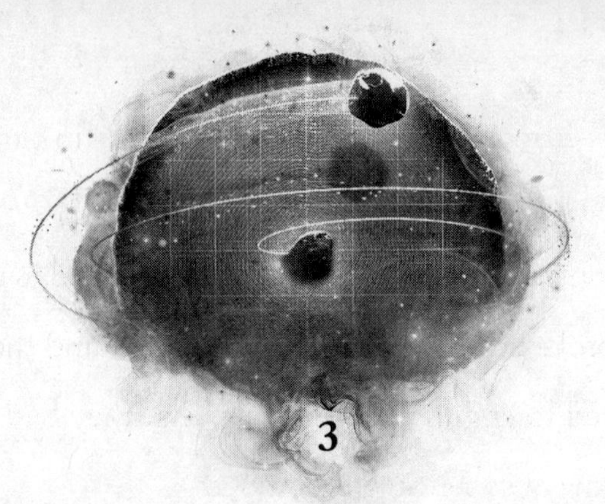

3

The Knights of Bithynia

A few houses down from their own, their little hedged-in lane gave way over a wooden stile to a spread of flat fenland, and Kay and Ell followed the loping strides of the two wraiths onto the frosted stubble. In the slow going of the garden and the tough brake and briars at the end of the lane, Kay had been stumbling, almost suspended between sleep and wake; now the sharp, frosted air of the fen hit her like a blast, and she looked, hunting and alert, for her sister's hand. Ell was still stumbling a bit, groggy and delicate after nearly tumbling from the low roof outside the back window. Kay dragged her on. Scrambling over a slick stile, she thought she had lost the wraiths completely; but then, ahead, a burst of something caught her eye—a low orange flame, it looked like—and she heard Flip's impatient voice.

"Come on!" he hissed. "No time! It's almost dawn!"

It only broke on her, as they came in closer and the dark of the sky seemed to engulf them entirely, that they had stepped into the shadow of something enormous.

"Quick—hop up and into the basket," Will said, putting out a hand.

In another sudden burst of orange flame, the entire scene was illuminated. Kay felt a surge of excitement and terror: the two wraiths had tethered a giant hot-air balloon to the frozen ground, and its massive lifting envelope towered above them in the cold and settling damp of the early morning. Kay's eyes were drawn by the burst of flame into the interior of the balloon, into the seemingly endless curve rising into the air. Ell had stopped dead and was pulling back on her arm.

Flip, by contrast, was all motion, scuttling around the balloon and hauling up the stakes that had kept the basket at tether. "No time, no time," he was feverishly muttering to himself, punctuated by heaves of effort as he dragged up at the long metal stakes and pushed down on the handle of a complicated-looking contraption he had fetched from its hook on the edge of the basket.

"We really are short on time," Will said insistently, now from the more-than-darkness left by the extinguishing of the flame. Ell was still trying to pull Kay backward, away. "We need to make height by dawn, or we'll be noticed. Wraiths are one thing," he said, now putting both his hands out over the lip of the basket to the two girls. "We're here, we're not here—but big colorful balloons in the sky attract attention. Come on, I'll help you up. Plenty of room inside."

"It's going to be okay. Really," said Kay.

Then, taking Ell in a warm hug and burying her face in the soft-brushed texture of her fleece, Kay promised that she would take care of her. She lifted her up toward Will, climbed easily into the basket herself and sat down hard on the floor, shutting her eyes against the quickly advancing light that would have shown her—had she turned her head—the end of her lane, the houses pale in the predawn and the streetlights—one, two, three—shining outside the window where their mother lay still asleep in her warm bed on Christmas morning. Kay gritted her teeth. She could hear Ell sobbing, and then felt the weight of her burying into the pit under her right arm. Flip must have been lighting the burner again, because she could feel on her face the heat and light of the huge flame, and hear the rush of the gas. And she could hear him winding winches and tightening the various halyards and straps on what sounded like a thousand cleats. Then, suddenly, there was a jolt, and she heard Flip call out from close by, "Almost!" And then there was a bang and a lot of grunting as the two wraiths hoisted themselves into position in the basket. Then silence.

For an instant Kay felt nothing but the tension in the whole frame of the balloon—the buoyancy of the bag above, straining to fly free of the cold earth, the hot charged air surging up into its envelope, the creaking in the thick, ancient-looking wooden boards of the basket floor as they seemed to be nearly torn asunder between the cables above and the last taut lines below. Just for an instant.

Kay only noticed that she had been holding her breath when it finally exploded from her—as the balloon broke from its last mooring and sprang into the air. Ell cried out into her side, and shook. Or perhaps that was the shuddering of the basket itself as it throbbed, then leaped into the slack of the cables, then settled again, making the whole balloon lurch sickeningly even as it shot up into the sky. Kay gasped and gasped.

She squeezed her eyes tight shut again, braced her leg against something hard and drove herself into the solid wood behind her. And then, after what seemed like a single unbroken and very tense moment, during which they might as well have been falling instead of rising, she felt something warm covering her lap, and she dared to crack an eye open.

"Here, pull this up to your chins," said Will as he tucked a heavy blanket round them where they huddled on the boards, under the hang of the basket's rim. The air rushing into their faces, even from their sheltered spot, was well beyond freezing; as cold as the questions that lay chill in Kay's mouth. She quickly drew the blanket up to and across their faces, putting her arm round her sister. Questions could wait.

She found it steadying to watch the two wraiths where they stood, out of reach, talking just beyond her hearing about comfortable things. Neither smiled, but their cheeks carried a composure and their eyes a lift and alertness that made their unheard words dance with welcoming possibility. Ell lay quiet, then asleep in the crook of her arm, and still Kay watched Will and Flip, the former with his lively, lithe limbs and slender, bow-like spring, the latter more solid but spry, a chunk of chestnut to Will's soaring lime. All the while the basket rose, at first quickly, but then, the gas slackening, far more slowly, bobbing into the currents of air that began to throw it eastward. When the lurch and tumble of the ascent had at last wholly settled, Kay heaved herself into a squat, tucked the blanket around Ell carefully and stood up.

The day was coming on fast, or maybe it had simply become lighter because they had climbed in the sky. In any case, the whole of the basket around her seemed suddenly to trip into the dawn. All around it dangled tools of every kind: wrenches, handles, mallets and hammers, tinderboxes and thick metal bars, long stakes and hoops, coils of rope in about twenty different thicknesses, extra hooks and clasps, spare cleats palely gleaming against the intermittent bursts from the wick, buckles and hasps, rings, a collection of keys, buckets of sand, and everywhere—of course—bags of ballast in various sizes. Kay could see the taut ropes running over the sides of the basket where Flip had, in the short time since they had taken off, already thrown out ballast. The thought of the bags swinging freely, then dropping through the air below the basket made her think of the height at which they must be traveling, and she felt suddenly queasy—queasy and sad. Home would be vanishing below them, behind them. She turned back to the center, trying to steady herself, fixing her eye on the floor, and tried to mark out the little things—Flip's sandals with their fine latticing of leather straps; a little wooden capstan with its iron handles at the bottom; and the dense console of instruments suspended from the main ring, hanging before Will in the very middle. Kay could see what looked like dials, which she guessed gave information on their altitude and speed or direction, their position. There were a few levers, and then, beside a long gray tube, the important nozzle that Flip kept adjusting, which must, Kay thought, release the gas into the balloon, catching its fire from the pilot flame burning on the wick.

So it did, she thought as it burst into orange flame. She would have jumped back, had there been anywhere to jump to. Flip caught her eye and smiled.

"Do you want to see the ocean?" said Will brightly.

In a couple of hesitant, slightly unsteady steps, she had joined the two wraiths at the wooden rim, crouching low into her own caution so that only her shoulders cleared the basket. She steadied herself, and then looked out.

Ahead—what was it?—slightly south of east, her father had told her—she could see the sun just about to crest the horizon. She couldn't tell if it was land or sea there, because it began to gleam and glare with its clear light; but there was definitely sea almost directly beneath them, green-gray in the paleness, with a strip of sheer white as it broke against the narrow sands of the Norfolk coast. Around and behind, the dark flats of the fens lay silver in the frost and early mist. Little houses broke up the fields, and every so often a line of streetlamps glowed orange for a while, and then sputtered out. Off to her left Kay could see the lights of a town paling in the onset of dawn, with a bit of coal smoke rising here and there—or at least she imagined it might have been coal smoke.

"Where are we going?" she said after a while. "Are we going to another world?"

Will stood beside her, hunched over with his elbows spread and his chin resting on the backs of his long fingers. He didn't look at her, but out into the long, level distance to the northeast, watching the sun break from the emerging line of the horizon. He was silent for a long time, but Kay knew that he had heard her so she kept her mouth shut. By the time he answered, Ell had awoken and was tentatively poking her head under Kay's left arm. The girls listened carefully as the land and ocean resolved and unfurled below them. It roared.

"So far as I know," Will said, the suspicion of a grin

turning up the corners of his mouth, "this is the only world there is. No," he continued slowly, as if to himself, "it's not so much *where* we're going as *how* we are getting there."

Kay was baffled by this, so after glancing down at her face, Will tapped his hand thoughtfully and percussively against the rail on the edge of the basket. Kay watched him. He looked out, as if at the distance, but also as if he were seeing something; something that hung in the empty space around the balloon. His eye darted in every direction, sometimes pausing for a moment but always moving on with the predictability and pattern—which is to say without either—of a butterfly in a summer garden. His gaze hovered and darted like a bird. It seemed almost to be touching things, so delicately, so deliberately did his pupil swivel, stop, focus and hold its position.

Below them the sea lay ridged and stippled, a booming voice calling silently from the bottom of an enormous well. Ell was silent, but had slipped her arm out of the blanket that still hung draped around her shoulders, and held her sister close by the waist. Kay felt her touch, still insistent with fear or anxiety, and thought about home slipping away behind them, the glowing streetlights being absorbed into the lesser brilliance of a cold December day, her mother just beginning to turn over in bed, wondering why it was so quiet in the house so late in the morning. Christmas morning. And all they had left her was a single scribbled note.

"In the old days," Will said, halfway through a breath, as if just taking up where he had left off, "we used to travel by sea. Out of Bithynia you could sail nearly anywhere, though of course it took time, more time than now, and naturally that meant we had to be much better organized. These days we rush. We tend to make more mistakes. But then, we have more to do, too."

From the other side of the basket Flip snorted, still sore, Kay reckoned, over that misplaced final page of the order sheet. Turning, she watched him through the rigging and gear where he paused over the board of meters and dials. He was mothering them, his face and attention completely fixed, his fingertips from time to time lightly brushing them. From the side she noticed his long, childlike lashes, a bloom of red around his cheekbones, his smooth skin, the impatient but somehow amused expression on his face. His crumpled, folded form seemed at one with the complex density of dials and levers positioned around him, as if he were their instrument as much as they were his. His concentration and his evident sense of comfort were infectious; Kay, dwelling on him, thought with pleasure that the balloon was flying him home, and all he was doing was letting it.

His home.

Her eyes lurched to Will's.

"But where are we going? Bithynia? Where's that?"

"No, we're not going to Bithynia," said Will, shaking his head almost imperceptibly. "The place we are going, in the mountains, doesn't have a name." Then he brightened slightly. "But we're going there in the right way. By the air, through the air."

"By the air, through the air," Flip intoned from a couple of meters away. He didn't look up.

"But why not Bithynia?" Kay couldn't let it drop, not after the events of the previous night. Not after Andrea Lessing. She looked directly at Will, holding his gaze like a foot stuck in a door. He didn't dare avoid her.

"Because the Bride is gone," he said simply, and got to his feet, keeping low but shifting quickly over to help Flip, who needed no help. Kay was certain she wasn't going to get any more than that. Nobody ever said more than that, more than those two words—the *Bride, Bithynia, Bithynia,* the *Bride.*

Unbidden but unavoidable, the memory of raised voices in the kitchen, only a week before, clanged in her head. The conversation never *went* anywhere. Bracing her shoulders against the cold air, Kay gritted her teeth and slumped down into the shelter of the blanket to join Ell, who quickly clipped her around the chest, holding her tight. Her eyes closed and, with the gentle swaying of the basket, Kay began to drift into a lightly nauseous doze. It was through this haze, at some distance, that she noticed Will taking up his answer again; groggy and warm, she listened, trying to catch the slow trickle of words.

"The Bride," he said from somewhere very near her ear, "of Bithynia. The queen of silk, the mulberry maid, touch to the torch hearts of ten thousand lovers, the only immortal. When I was a boy, before all this, I saw her once, fleetingly, below our house in the valley, in among the plantations, passing on her way to the sea at dusk. Whenever I think of it, of her, I can still feel on my face the damp weight of the air that evening, like a tiny bristling chill on the skin above my lips. Everything that reminds me of her goes through me like a spear."

There was silence then, or rather a rushing drone like a low howl. Kay felt the spear all right, remembering the sharp, pointed voices of her parents bouncing off the close walls of the little kitchen; the cold, hardened looks. In her mind's eye, as the wind bristled and arched its back, she could see her father slumped where he stood, taking it, taking the criticism, as if he were a victim, as if he were just a misunderstood but patient hero. He had his bag slung over his shoulder, and his coat was on; he stood by the door that led out to the hallway, though he made no move to go. "She's a bride, after all—why don't you marry *her*?" There was never anything he could say to that.

But Will was in another world. "There was a man in my village," he said, "an old man, half blind, who fought for the Bride in the east, back when he was young, before the trading route was opened, before he had lost the use of his legs. He would sit by day on a mat outside his door, in the shade of a massive cedar, and recite the stories he had learned along the way: of her miraculous delivery out of the foam of the sea, of her Acquisition of the Nine Forms, of the Great Marriage. And if you waited long enough and listened quietly, he might tell the prophecy of her passing, too."

Kay nodded heavily, as if she, and not the heavy rocking of the basket in the forewind that drove it, were moving her head. Her consciousness seemed to swim sidelong with the motion of her lolling temples, and she thought of opening her eyes. Eye.

She couldn't remember how many eyes she had, but then, just now she didn't need to see anyway.

The prophecy of her passing, she thought. Passing.

"Her passing out of this world," Will said finally and softly; but both girls were fast asleep.

By the time Kay woke, everything was different. For one thing, it was dark again. But the air was dry, too, and bitterly cold, as sharp on her bones as cut glass. Ell had crumpled to one side, and lay lightly snoring; to her other side Kay found the wraiths close, sitting opposite one another as they played some game on a large board between them. They stared at little black stones and from time to time, without really taking turns, they moved them.

"Where are we going?" asked Kay abruptly.

I still don't know.

Will picked up one of the stones and gripped it in his hand. He seemed startled, then relaxed. "We're going to see Sergeant Ghast about your father. We're going to do something about all this witnessing."

"And authoring," added Flip. He checked a meter and gave the balloon a long pulse of flame.

"But where . . ." Kay threw out her hand to take in the black void around the balloon, through which she could only dimly see a rough, dry expanse of crag and scrub slowly passing beneath them as the wind drove the balloon ever on. "Where is all this? Where are we now?"

"Everything flows down from the mountains," said Will. His head lay a little to one side, and he looked at her as if she were an object of great happiness. Every word he said to her he seemed to think a privilege. "As with water, so it is also with stories. If we want to get to the start of this one, we have to go up and into the mountain."

Kay could feel her blood rising. "You're not answering me," she said. Flat, but not sullen.

"There *is* no answer, really," said Will. "Or at least, not the kind of answer you want. At first you may feel disappointed, but in your frustration there is, too, perhaps, a little ground of hope." He looked down at the board before him, at the shining black stones, and moved first one then another, the first simply and curtly, the second in a long arc. "There are times when what is most important is glimpsed—*can only* be glimpsed—in the dark. There are times when any mountain will do, when it is important that one goes into *a* mountain rather than *the* mountain, *this particular* mountain. We are going to such a place, in such a way, to see a thing that lies higher than other things."

Kay wanted to be furious, but with every word Will spoke a little more of her frustration seemed to slip from her. Because he wasn't ignoring her—quite the opposite. His eyes passed back and forth between her and the board on which his hand still rested, almost as if it were a canvas and he were painting her portrait.

"I don't understand," she said. "I don't understand at all."

"Good," said Flip. He was crouching nearer to her, and could reach out his hand and touch her arm. The feel of it, the gentle squeeze near her shoulder—avuncular, delicate strength—buoyed and inflated her. "Knowing that you don't understand is good. It's usually when people think they understand, when they're so sure of themselves, that they're dead wrong."

"But who is Ghast? And what does he want with my father?"

Will and Flip both stared at the board before them.

"What is he going to do with him?"

"Will," said Flip, so quietly that Kay could barely hear him. "She is young, but—"

"She is in danger."

"She is an *author*. She has come very far already, and very bravely."

Will sat back a bit, his arms still hugging his knees and pulling them up off the floor of the basket. "To tell you who Ghast is, I need to tell you the story of the knights of Bithynia."

Bending his head over the board where he and Flip had been playing, Will began to move the small pieces—rounded stones, Kay now saw, oblong in shape, of a grayish-blue cast, like the pebbles she sometimes gathered on the Norfolk coast. They swirled in patterns around the board, his long, delicate fingers stirring without pause, independently of one another in continuous curves, loops and eddies. At the end of each finger, at any given moment, one, or two, or a few stones were being gently pushed or pulled, so that Kay could see upon the board a pattern of movement being described in time, the stones collecting together, fanning apart, organizing into groups, trading elements, reconstituting and recombining, then all severing again, constantly changing their distribution across the face of the board. At first this movement bewildered her, and she thought in frustration that she would just turn round, crawl back through the rigging and rejoin Ell beneath the warm blanket. But as she kept watching, she saw that one of the stones was moving differently from the others, and she began to think there might be method to Will's movements. This one stone made short, jerky lurches, mostly in straight lines, though it was passed from finger to finger in the process, and for that reason, its motion was not obvious to her at first. As she watched, it was hit repeatedly by the other stones, and she thought that it must be a very sorry stone to be the victim of so many collisions; but it seemed rather that it was drawing these other stones to it—not least because these, after each hit, seemed to lurch away from the encounter with some of its character, interrupting their more graceful arcs around the board with increasingly stilted movements. As Will's fingers continued to weave around the board, Kay began not to notice them at all, and could see only the lives of the stones: the way this one, like a virus, began to infect all the others with its short, jerking stutter, as if it were berating them for their beauty and making them ashamed. Kay's head tightened, and she felt her chin thrusting forward as she tried to swallow a sob.

"Will, stop."

It was Flip, placing his hand over the board and silencing Will's fingers, who brought Kay back to her senses.

"She can read it," he said. "You're shouting at her. Stop it."

On the board Flip's hand tightened, his knuckles white as if he were pushing against Will's fingers with enormous force.

Kay looked up at Flip, but Will didn't acknowledge him at all; he simply allowed Flip to steady his hand, and began speaking in so quiet a voice that Kay struggled to hear him above the intense thrill of the wind around them.

"For centuries we were a guild, the thousand and one of us, every wraith an equal voice in the halls of Bithynia, each a knight. The left-wraiths, their hands full of stones, plotted the causes, the effects and the ways of things, seeing the world and all who dwell in it as a tissue of stories and narratives, skein on skein of causation and consequence; while the right-wraiths, with their palms stretched open to the inspiration of the air, of dreams, imagined a universe of ideas, dreaming and conjuring, tireless in their grand frenzies of vision. Together we sailed with the wind, weaving up the edges of the earth with our songs. Those were days of power, when the left-wraiths, great bards and tellers of tales, drew from the right-wraiths, from the imaginers and prophets, the matter and grounds for the most magical fables, for epics and romances that sprawled across the continents and encompassed the seven seas. We lived and turned in a kind of balance then, a poised and perfect motion. The plotters revered the imaginers, and the imaginers in turn deferred to the plotters. We seemed to move in a kind of dance without end, and our figures spilled out from our halls, and washed the world in story—"

"Those days were long ago, old friend," said Flip. With a gentle gesture, as if he were setting down a delicate, valuable thing upon a precarious surface, he let go of Will's hand where it lay on the board between them.

"We were happy. Maybe we were too innocent. But we were happy." Will spoke as though from far away, and Kay thought the basket was too small to contain the vast void between them. "We had worked by the board for a thousand years. But then the balance suddenly seemed to shift, and Ghast—"

"Who took my father," said Kay.

"Who took your father," agreed Will. "Ghast isn't really a plotter. He hates imaginers. His is a voice not so much of story or tale, neither of means nor of motion, not imaginer, nor plotter, not visionary nor spell-spinner. Ghast is more—he is a force for—"

"For results," put in Flip quietly. "Ghast is motivated only by power—the creation of power, the development of power, the unyielding grip on power. He doesn't care for stories. He doesn't care for telling or for seeing. He cares nothing for friendship, nothing for beauty. He wants profit. Profit and power. From the very beginning, power was all Ghast ever wanted."

Will nodded. "Power, yes. He seemed to be clotting around himself more and more of the left-wraiths. It began to appear that they were actually taking orders from him and not, as formerly, working by the board. And they were moving toward Ghast. Over time Ghast attracted more of the left-wraiths, and then, gradually, even some right-wraiths, too, until there were so many of them that they dared to put the guild to a vote—and we lost it. And Ghast was made Sergeant of the new order, and now we take that order from him."

"Except when that order happens to be on page nineteen of a sheet you wiped your nose with," said Flip.

"Yes," agreed Will, but he wasn't listening.

Flip rolled his eyes merrily at Kay, but he decided that she wasn't listening, either. So Flip got to his feet, climbed over Kay to the instruments and began fussing with the ropes and valves, checking his dials and muttering to himself as he checked off items on a mental checklist.

Kay stared hard at the board lying before her; at its

irregular, unfinished border, its dark, stained surface that still showed the grain of the tree from which it had been cut, at the sheen that flared from it as the lantern swung unsteadily above. She was quickly spellbound, watching where Will's fingers now continued circulating absentmindedly, their tips brushing, nudging the stones against the occasional thuds and jolts of the basket in its forward swing. She could see something new in Will's patterns, something strange that she felt should not have been there: two stones at the center—one almost silent and still, but nudged at regular intervals like the tick of a clock; the other extravagant, sweeping in spontaneous arcs, impulsive, lucky. She felt instinctively that she was the first, that her sister was the second. She knew it as surely as if Will had taken out a brush and colors, and painted their portraits.

Kay looked up to Will. "What is this board?" she asked. "What are these stones? Is it a game?"

Will frowned. "No, not a game. Not exactly a game. There is no contest here, no winner or loser—just movement and reading. It's called a plotting board, and these are plotting stones. No left-wraith will travel without them; they are always with us. It gives us a way to reduce any story, any situation, any narrative to its simplest elements so that we can see its structure and understand how what is happening now is connected to what has come before, and how what is happening now will lead to other situations and stories in the future."

"So this is a way of predicting the future? Can you tell me what's going to happen to me? Can you see if we'll find our father?"

"No. That's prophesying. That's different; there are wraiths who do it, but they don't do it with plotting boards. They pluck visions out of the air as the eye does stars on a cold night. With plotting boards we just look at the shapes of stories and try to understand the way those shapes work. It's about probabilities, patterns, habits, the way things *are most likely* to turn out. For example, the stone you saw before was Ghast, and the stones around it some of the other wraiths; and I think the interactions between this stone and the others you saw showed the way Ghast came to relate to them, began to exert influence on them, made them into images of himself."

Kay nodded, wishing that the blackish-bluish stones, now so still but for the occasional nudging, would swirl back again into their finger-driven dance, gliding across the surface of the mottled board.

"And afterward, that stone was me," she said, touching it, "and this one was Ell."

Will looked at her sharply, as if she had stung him.

"Or not," she offered. "Maybe I was wrong."

"No," he answered, softening. His fingers danced again on the board. "There are many ways of seeing any particular movement. The shape made by a stone, like any symbol, can stand for many things. For instance, the tension I showed you might also be the relation between order and randomness. Or you might see that movement as the spread of disease, communicating itself between, say, mice in a den or rabbits in a warren, and in time contaminating the whole group. There are as many interpretations of that structure as you have time to evolve them; but I told you it was Ghast, and so you saw Ghast."

"But is what you do on the board true?" Kay was groping for something, but she wasn't sure what.

"Models, thoughts and stories are always true. What you do with them is a different thing."

At that moment there was a lurch, and Flip—who had been muttering—began to bark and then to shout. Will leaped to a low squat, his head suddenly, carelessly tangled in the rigging, his long fingers clutching at the air. Everything clashed around them, instruments swinging, tumbling, colliding and breaking as the basket leaped wildly through the sky.

They were falling.

Before she could register what Flip was saying, Kay was halfway back to the rear of the basket, skirting round toward Ell, who, roused with the jolt and the noise, blinked with terror into the gray-black of the night. Will fell down to the floor to haul on a winch, and Flip furiously released gas into the envelope of the balloon—trying, Kay guessed, to create lift in the nauseating plunge of free fall. For a long while she felt as if she were bouncing, weightless, on the moon. Her arms were around Ell when she finally made sense of Flip's shouting: "By the *air*!" he cried, willing them to rise, willing them to sail. "Through the *air*!"

Just before they crashed, Kay remembered what she had seen, sitting at that plotting board as the commotion began: a single, graceful stone still arcing untouched and alone around the margins of the knotted board—slowly, but elegantly, spinning.

"There was a crash."

They clustered and shifted before him, long and light forms scarcely able to hold their shape against his squat solidity.

"How many dead?"

"None."

"None yet."

With sudden decision, he strode forward. They parted to let him through, like oil before water, then closed in behind him.

"We must prepare a welcome. See that everything is made ready for them, and for the girl. We must bring our new plans forward."

The nearest, being the most servile as well as the most ambitious, saw his opportunity.

"We have plotted it on the board, and—"

"This is no time to prattle of your grandmother's superstitions. Not to me." The rebuke was total, even as the stride unbroken. "The old thread is cut. You are my servants now, and I will have none of your stones and swirling sorceries here."

They passed in a little group into a large and open hall. Ghast took the center and spun around slowly. He held his knotted stubs of hands up to the vast reach of the room.

"Call me your master. The master of all this."

"You are the only master in the mountain."

"Mine is the only hand that can command. Mine is the only fist. And yet I am not the only master."

In the hall a hundred lights were lighted.

"Be gentle with the girl. She is a means to my end. And with her sister—however it falls out." He waved his hand in annoyance. "But as for the other, spare neither strokes nor speeches. Net him about with lies. He must break, and soon."

4

GHAST

If the flying had been cold and turbulent, if it had seemed sometimes difficult and nauseating, the sudden final descent of the balloon—though short—was far worse. Kay's stomach heaved into the tips of her fingers, and her throat, dry and knotted like the gall of an oak, choked her. She almost felt relief when, after a few seconds, the basket crashed into what sounded like rocky ground. In a slow havoc it began to drag, splinter and throb all at once. The envelope of the balloon continued to deflate, and pulled first rigging then cloth all around them. Flip must have put out the fire, she thought, because for the first time since the morning it was pitch-dark. Time moved so slowly that Kay felt oddly as if she had a lot of time to think as she gripped Ell to her, groping for air with a free hand and continuing to wedge herself into the cavity under the basket's rim. She caught some breath and gradually felt the terrible forward crushing of the basket come to a full stop. And then all was quiet.

As she groped a little more with her hand, she found a pocket of air that had come from a tear in the balloon fabric. Releasing Ell, she reached for the tear, pulling it as close as she could amid the folds and tangled mass of the material. Then, latching her sister close, she heaved the two of them up toward it. With some struggling, they got their faces free, then out into the night air. She could see almost nothing past a couple of meters. The moon was hidden, and there was no sign of Will or Flip.

"Ell, are you okay?" Kay relaxed her arm a little, but the slight body of her sister remained firmly pressed to her side.

The voice might have been muffled, but it came out strong. "I can't get my legs free." Eloise sounded as if she were trying to solve a puzzle—rather than extricate herself from the aftermath of a terrifying crash. Kay felt her heart loosen at the simple, courageous statement.

After some pushing and wriggling, Kay disentangled them both from the heavy swaddle of the cloth. They found themselves standing on it, unsteadily attempting to cross its still billowing surface toward the edge, and firmer ground. The thick-draped darkness around them ruffled with the breeze. Under Kay's hand, where the sleeve of her coat had hiked up in the crash, the skin of Ell's arm suddenly broke out in goose pimples.

"Kay," she said, her little voice still resonant with innocent courage, "what's happened? I thought we were going to find Dad."

Even if there had been time to answer, Kay wouldn't have known what to say. But she didn't, and there wasn't.

"Jump off. Quickly," said Will, his face looming out of the darkness, weirdly lit by the raking light of a bright lantern. "It's not safe. Grab on. Now."

Kay hauled at Ell and tried to fling her forward. She herself only just had time to lurch and then topple onto Will as a piece of the tackle and rigging sprang airward, lashing into the place where she had been standing the instant before. At last she saw Flip, with a long knife in his hand, sawing at something. He was cutting a cable.

"We came down on a cliff," Will said in a low voice. He was just audible over the rising wind. "I tried to get an anchor in, but it won't hold the basket if the sailcloth goes over and catches the wind. And it is. Going over. Flip's trying to save the basket. What's left of it."

Just behind them the basket lay turned on its side. Taut cables stretched past them, tense with the strain of the balloon's fabric, which was taking the heavy gusts and pulling the whole rig down a slope toward—toward what might have been a cliff. Beneath their feet lay dry, rocky ground; a few feet further on, large boulders and plinths of stone stood heaped in irregular formations.

Flip was moving around the now nearly upended basket, working his way through the ropes and cables, which snapped and flung away as he sheared them. He had four or five to go when he called out to Will, "Move the girls back in case anything gets fouled."

Will pulled Kay, and Kay reached out to grab Ell's hand. She started to pull her toward the shelter of a cluster of large stones. But Ell wasn't coming. Kay tugged.

"Kay," said the strong little voice behind her. "Kay, I think I'm stuck again."

Everything seemed to happen in a slow rush. She turned, and by Will's light immediately saw that her sister's leg had become snagged in a mass of halyards, guy ropes, tethers, sailcloth and other debris from the balloon's crash. But no sooner had she turned than Ell's hand was wrenched from her own and her tiny form dragged two or three meters across the hard ground. The movement of the fabric in the wind, billowing in places like a sail, twisted and flipped her little body as it dragged her, with every meter tangling her further in a tight knot of cords and fabric. She was screaming.

"Kay! My foot is tangled, Kay!" Her shrill screams lashed through the gusty air like snapping cables.

Flip had sprung clear the instant the balloon shifted. At first he was watching only his own feet, keeping himself free, while Kay stood stunned, paralyzed, staring at him, willing him to help. And Will—she felt like the three of them were standing deep underwater; for a moment everything seemed so heavy.

Then Ell began sliding toward the edge of the cliff face again.

They all reached her at about the same time—Flip bounding across the dancing ropes like some sort of deranged and acrobatic snake charmer, Will loping low along the ground, grabbing at the ropes where he could, trying to get purchase on something—anything—to stop the balloon's relentless drag toward the cliff's edge. But Kay had eyes only for Ell, and it was to her outstretched arms that she ran, without any thought that her own feet might become snared as the tackle lashed and swirled around her ankles like so many vicious and venomous jaws.

"Kay, help me! Help!" cried Ell. She was sobbing with frustration, pushing and squirming against the ropes binding her. Kay hooked her fingers around one fragile wrist, then the other. She held, fighting Ell to be quiet, to stay put. She wanted to tell her not to squirm, not to struggle and by struggling to engage herself still further in the tightening coils. Will had his hands on something—a section of fabric—and had dug his heels against the loose stones lying all around; with a heaving effort he was holding back the weight of the cloth, buying the little girl time.

"Just hold it, Will," called Flip. He was near. He had Ell's leg in his hands. It was wrapped in cords and leather straps. The leg of her trousers had been pulled up and her calf was starting to turn purple. Kay stared at it. There were so many knots, so many different strands and threads and turns and twists. Her eyes ached to see it, and the blood in her chest crawled against her ribs like ants.

"Use your knife, Flip—I can't hold it," Will called out.

Flip was still staring at Ell's leg, at the mass of knots and tangles. "I can't—there's too much. I'd cut her. Wait."

"I can't wait, Flip. If the wind rises—"

Flip backed away and stood up. A mass of fury screamed in Kay's head. *How dare he give up! How dare he walk away!*

"Kay. Kay. Kay."

Flip's hands were dancing before his face, writhing with his fingers extended, looking intently at Ell, then at his hands, then at Ell. Kay thought at first that he was going to cast some sort of spell, that he thought he was some kind of sorcerer—but that wasn't it. He was moving his hands in the way Will had earlier over the plotting board.

"Three more seconds, Flip," said Will. He spat every word through a separate surge of exhausted effort. Kay could see the strength, like the seconds, slipping from him.

Flip's hands danced. He seemed mesmerized now, as if he had entranced himself, as if he were watching the most important thing in the world, as if he had become so engaged and enthralled with it that he had fallen out of time, as if he were deep in a kind of intent love with the movement of his hands in the air before him. He seemed as tangled as Ell.

And then, suddenly, he snapped out of it. With a fluid motion, he reached to the knife at his belt, drew it, dropped to his knees and sliced a single cord at the top left of the mass of knots that were still tightening around Ell's knee and thigh. At the same moment Will, exhausted, let slip the cloth from his fists and fell backward, toppling across Flip's shoulder and knocking him flat on the ground.

But Kay hardly noticed.

She only had eyes for the cords around Ell's leg. They seemed to recoil from the place where Flip had cut, as if they were living things. Some spun and whipped away; others swirled and untwisted like water pouring down a drain; others again seemed to untie themselves from complex knots and vanish like steam on a breeze—but one way or another, as if a key had turned with a click in its lock, they all sped off, and Ell scrambled to her feet and launched her body into Kay's arms. Kay just held her.

How did he do that?

By the time she opened her eyes again and looked around, the two wraiths had already set about sorting the salvage. Flip was hauling carefully at the basket—upended a few meters away—and, with a tottering crash, set it upright again. Kay scrutinized him over Ell's huddled shoulder. The thought flashed through her mind that he was dangerous; a thought that made her feel guilty when he looked up and caught her in it.

"Sometimes you just need to know which thread to cut," he said. He held her eyes the space of a long breath, shrugged and then clambered into the basket, checking for damage. "Not bad!" he called out.

After some hesitation and on unsteady legs, Kay and Ell followed to where Will stood.

"Instruments? Gear?" he was asking. "Can you get our position?"

"The good news," Flip said, practically beaming, "is that we're pretty much there. An hour's walk or less, I'd say. And the way the balloon collapsed onto the basket as we fell seems to have kept most of the gear in."

"Is there bad news?" asked Kay. The fall through the air, the terror of watching Ell dragged toward the cliff edge—it was too much. Her strength seemed to have drained away. She felt blank, as stunned as her sister's gaping eyes.

Flip was crouched and clattering in the bottom of the

basket. "The bad news is that we're going to have to carry whatever we want to keep. And if we want to have any hope of . . . that is, if we're to arrive in time—"

"We'll hurry," said Will. "Can you girls run?"

Ell was still rubbing her leg where the ropes had strangled it. Of course they were not going to run, Kay thought; but they both nodded.

They each took something: Will and Flip a few brown sacks, which looked heavy; Kay a little bag that Flip had filled hastily with a few instruments, the plotting board and the stones the girls had found scattered across the rocky ground; and Ell a small pile of blankets. Flip had some flares in the basket, and he lit one immediately, hoping that someone might see it and come for them, but also because, he said, the light it shed as it went up would give them a good sense of the landscape around them. The balloon had deposited them on a flat sort of plain high in the mountains; to one side there was a cliff, to the other a gentle downslope that, across a shallow valley, arced up toward a high peak. If they continued just a bit, they could get into a higher valley full of scrub and low trees, Will thought. There, they might get their bearings.

As they walked, the cloud started to break up above, and

before long, the light of the stars and the moon gave them surer footing as they carefully picked out a way down. By the time they were properly among the low bushes, they could see each other and the land around them much more easily. Kay held on to Ell at a little distance as Flip put up another flare, and in its showering light, they thought they briefly saw movement across the valley.

"That'll be Sprite and Jack"—Will grinned at Flip—"or I'm not a left-wraith."

Flip went on ahead, bounding in spite of his heavy sack, and Will nudged the girls along. Kay shifted her bag back and forth from her right side to her left, shouldering the burn and the ache of it. She shuffled her feet a little faster so it might seem like she was in fact running. It wasn't long before they could hear animated voices ahead, growing louder, and then, all of a sudden, in an orange glow that popped—like a water-light—from behind a bush, Kay and Ell saw Flip. He was with two other wraiths, like Will tall, gaunt and tapered. They were doling out the contents of Flip's sack into two others. Will immediately stopped, too, and offered his arm to his friends.

"Sprite," he said, beaming. The wraith took his arm in a two-handed, crossed grip, and briefly bound it to him hard, like a spar being lashed to a mast. Will turned to the other wraith, who was standing expectantly to greet him. "Jack of the Lantern," he cried. "We'll need your light tonight, my friend."

Jack took Will's arm in the same curious two-handed hold. All four wraiths then stood quietly, a kind of hum hanging between them, an energy, until they bent again to work. Kay knew that stillness, that taking pleasure in the moment, in silence, before allowing it to pass—for she had longed for it, imagined it and tried herself to create it so many times. Looking at the wraiths, she realized with surprise that it was love.

Will stooped, and began to divide up some of his own load. Kay was thinking how heavy their sacks must have been, and how resolute they had been, carrying them, when she saw what they contained.

"Those are my father's things," she stated. She was angry, and knew she had been too blunt.

Will's hands stopped moving, and the other wraiths—she could see them very clearly now that they inclined to her, with their round eyes, elegantly angular noses, high cheeks and feathery silvered hair—loomed inquisitively over their sacks.

It was Will who spoke, and he was awkwardly formal.

"I explained to you—ma'am—that we're removers, and we remove. We came to your house with our inventory, and we removed what we were instructed to remove. Down to the last tooth." His eyes met hers, and he smiled. As Kay realized what he was doing, she smiled, too, grudgingly. "Whether we like it or not—and I promise you that we don't—these days this is our job."

"Ma'am," said Flip with a sarcastically exaggerated bow. He rolled his eyes. Will had an impressively long and spiky elbow, and Kay reckoned it probably hurt Flip a lot when it was jabbed into his side.

But the others—Will had called them Sprite and Jack—were whispering to each other now. Will, like Kay, had seen their curiosity and, holding Kay's gaze, he added loudly, commanding their attention, "Yes, you heard me. We've got two little girls here who are more than they seem. And one of them"—he suppressed a smile, or a look of pride, beneath the serious, level intensity of the announcement as he continued—"is an author."

The others were as dumbfounded as Will and Flip had been and, though they said nothing, they shared furtive looks from time to time as Kay and Ell helped distribute the clothes and papers and books, and the other tiny familiar objects from sack to sack. And when the girls set off, surrounded by the four looming figures, the wraiths kept looking. Ell lagged quickly, and Sprite had to take the blankets over his shoulders, but Kay drew her on, encouraging and cajoling, at times pleading with her, at times roughly dragging her by the arm. Once, when her exhausted body had become nothing but a dead and sagging weight, Kay stopped and clasped her sister's pale face to her chest, willing the warmth to flood out of her and into the shivering, tiny form.

"Kay," said Ell, pushing back with surprising force, "I thought we were coming to find Dad. Instead all we're doing is helping to get rid of him." She dropped her last remaining little sack on the ground and began to sob.

It was all Kay could do to calm her sister's tears; after that she had no strength left to try to answer the questions that still whirled in the windy air around them: *What are they doing? Where is our father? What is all this for?* Jack took Ell on his back, and bore her cheerfully enough, but Kay carried on her shoulders only questions.

In less than an hour, having climbed out of the valley, then skidded down a loose scree of heavy rounded rocks and pebbles, they all put down their things outside what seemed to Kay an intolerably forbidding cave.

"Here we are," said Will, squatting down again to talk to the girls. Seeing Kay's tension, he added, "Don't be afraid. It's not like any cave you've imagined being in before."

And it wasn't: as Sprite and Jack breached the opening, their torch held aloft, a thousand other similar staffs fixed to the walls around a broad interior hall began to glow. Nor was it really a cave in anything but name: the walls of the cavernous domed room had been polished until they gleamed, and around it hung tapestries woven of the most extraordinary threads: golds, deep purples, crimsons, blues and yellows as striking as sharp notes, whites more brilliant than the walls themselves. Kay had seen medieval tapestries in old chapels and museums—not only at home, but also in the countless smaller towns and villages through which her father, with his endless itineraries (and notebooks, and cameras), had thought to drag them. Those tapestries had always seemed washed out, mostly a grayish blue or green, and while sometimes of enormous size, invariably they depicted the most boring subjects: victories in forgotten battles, a forest scene, another Madonna and child. But these tapestries were of another kind entirely—luminous, richly vibrant hangings, portraits that fascinated the eye with pictures of passion, danger, suffering, triumph and joy.

Kay's eyes roved hungrily. In one scene, she saw a hero plunging into a live volcano; next to it, two friends lying in a sea of sunflowers; in another, three nymphs emerging from a huge and flooding river, chased by porpoises; in others, angry or cheering faces; a choir of boys processing down a yawning Gothic nave; pirates in a slowly capsizing ship; and of course wraiths and gods and dwarfs and fairies, elves, satyrs, giants and monsters. Everywhere Kay looked, these almost moving images abutted one another, and seemed to create a static dance of texture, of color, of story.

Ell, too, was clearly stirred to wonder by the tapestries. All evidence of her exhaustion had vanished: though her arms hung limp at her sides, her face—angled up to the walls above—danced with excitement, interest and recognition. She turned, and turned. Her eyes floated over the pictures. Kay studied her for a moment, surprised at her concentration and the sudden bravery of her gaze after so much timid clinging throughout the last day. She stood alone in the long vaulted room, having stepped away from the others. Will and Flip were talking in low excitement with two other wraiths who had just come through from a far door as Kay took it all in. Her sister's red hair hung wispily, at last fully unraveled from the tight plait that Kay had woven in her curls the day before. The crash of the balloon had torn the hem of her blue duffel coat, something like grease had stained the leg of her trousers; but otherwise she seemed remarkably unmarked by the day's frenetic events; even Ell's face seemed to Kay relaxed, rested. She had an air of composure that Kay had never before seen in her, not even in sleep. It was as if Ell felt for the first time in her life completely at home.

"Kay," she said, turning, "I've dreamed about this place, I think. I know these pictures. I know these colors."

"That's impossible, Ell. You've never been here before, so you couldn't know anything about them." Kay was surprised to find herself speaking in an impatient tone.

"I know that. But what I mean is, I *feel* like I do." Ell pointed to a long, low tapestry hanging on the left wall, in which an old man, wizened with age but still brawny and somehow full of majesty, sat enthroned on a ledge. He was looking out on a small group of men who were approaching, bareheaded and in rags, from a shadowy corner in a great gray hall, so dimly lit that Kay thought it looked like granite, like the inside of a mountain. "I think I know—or I feel, anyway," Ell said, "what's happening in each one. Like that one over there—that old man is a judge, the judge of people's lives, their whole lives, after death. And the men coming to him are people who have just died. And they're going to their life after death, and the judge will tell them where to go—to heaven or hell. Kay, they're all like that. They just seem familiar, like they're pictures from a book we have at home. Or like I made them up myself."

"But, Ell, you know we don't have these pictures in a book." Something about her sister's urgency and conviction unsettled Kay, and made her irritable. "Just keep shush, and do what I do."

As she looked around, she noticed Jack and Sprite had gone, and Flip with them; meanwhile Will was speaking in increasingly animated whispers to the two other wraiths. Kay looked at him critically. In the bright light of the hall he looked even more insubstantial than earlier. Though his features and limbs were every bit as elegant as those of the others, he looked a bit more gaunt, a bit more bent. The others didn't have that tired, if cheerful, wryness to their cheeks. Instead the crescent moon of their faces had a sort of heavy crease, as if, had they been creatures chiseled in stone outside a cathedral, the sculptor had saved the deepest cuts and sharpest lines for their severe brows, their pursed lips, their grave chins. One of them was waving a handful of papers at Will. Kay immediately felt sorry for him—it had to be the inventory, she thought; and, sure enough, in a moment all three wraiths, after a short and tense silence, turned to her. Will came up first and, with his usual stooping grace, dropped to his haunches.

"Kay, I need to ask you for that tooth now. Foliot and Firedrake"—and here he gestured at the two looming caricatures of officiousness behind him—"they have to clear the removal with Sergeant Ghast, and Ghast doesn't like his officers to keep him waiting."

Something about the way he said "officers"—with a little hesitation, maybe—made Kay distrust these new wraiths. She avoided looking up at them, instead holding Will's eyes. There she found comfort and, in the face of this new threat, which she felt instinctively was dangerous to him as well as to her, resoluteness. "Tell them, please, that I will take it to Ghast myself."

Foliot and Firedrake had been listening. Now they tittered mirthlessly and crumpled the papers into a ball just behind Will's head; but he stayed put, and Kay thought she saw another smile at the corner of his eyes. She felt Ell's duffel coat brush up against her, and reached out to hold her hand, still not breaking Will's gaze. He never looked away. A long moment seemed to open, long enough for Kay to decide—for certain—that whatever he said, she would trust him. Finally he said, "So. I will go with you, and I will be your guide." He breathed out and nodded. "You'll need one."

There followed a whirl of motion, so brisk and startling that Kay couldn't take it all in. Will strode lightly along beside the girls, following Foliot and Firedrake. He was clearly paying close attention to the response of Ghast's emissaries. They must, Kay judged, be Will's superiors: he followed them, and his eye seemed so fixed on each detail of their movement, each articulation of their glances one to the other, that she dared not interrupt his focus.

As they passed through the door at the end of the hall, the lights behind them darkened even as the lights before them blazed. Had Kay never dreamed dreams; had her father not carried her on his shoulders through half the cathedrals in England, lifting her as high as he could to see if, just this once, she might touch the roof; had she not on summer evenings lain with Ell in the waste field behind their lane, their heads pillowed by a clump of clover, singing songs to put the otherwise lethargic clouds into a dance across the vault of the sky—then she might not have been struck by the room—the cavern—into which the wraiths then led them. But she *had* dreamed, and reached, and sung, and she knew the size of this place, upon which the light of a thousand, or ten thousand, torches suddenly spilled in a concert of discovery. Kay had learned to look up.

It was a library; or, more accurately, a great treasure hall of books. If one were to take the greatest domes, and naves, and halls, and chambers, the grandest throne rooms, and amphitheaters, the largest of arenas, and combine them, this colossal cavern would be the result. The shelves on which the countless books stood had been carved from the rock of the cave. Along the floor, on carpets woven in wine and violet, long tables had been laid in aisles, on which here and there a plotting board sat, a pile of stones at the edge of each one. She counted four—no, five—aisles. Through the hall, gigantic globes of the earth and moon and stars stood mounted in wooden casings, and low stools were tucked in an orderly way beneath each of the tables—enough for, Kay reckoned, about a thousand wraiths. She couldn't get a close look at any of the books themselves, but she could see plainly that some of them—even, perhaps, most of them—were a thousand pages each, or more. Above, the shelves rose toward the vault and the books grew smaller, so tiny at the top that she wasn't even sure, from this distance, that they were books. It was more than her eyes could compute, much less her head.

At the far end of the hall, a little door led to a stairway cut into the rock, which rose to a balconied room that overlooked the library. In a wide space beneath this balcony, the tables had been so arranged to make room for a strange metal disk, about a dozen feet in diameter and set into the floor, in which smiths had cut with fine tools intricate embellishments adorned with precious gems. As they passed, Foliot and Firedrake strode without care over this gorgeous, gold-leafed disk, a kind of sacrilege that Ell, encountering it, was unable to imitate. Entranced by the color and workmanship of the circle, she came to a full halt.

"It's very beautiful," said Will, drawing up to stand beside her. Among the swirling shapes and symbols he pointed out elaborate representations of the moon in different phases, and little rubies cut to show like the buds of flowers opening, that seemed to catch something of the color of Ell's hair.

"What is it?" Kay asked. She was prodding with her

foot at the disk's edge a dark, circular hole, one of many that circled it.

"It's a clock," said Ell matter-of-factly. Will brightened for the first time in hours.

"In a way, yes," he said. "We call it the Great Wheel. When the Honorable Society holds its annual festival, once a year, we mark the days by turning it, one turn for every day. There—" He gestured at the hole that Kay was still prodding with her foot. "Those holes are for long iron staves, one staff for each of the twelve holes, and—"

The two officious wraiths had reappeared in the far door, and one of them—Foliot, Kay thought—stamped his foot once, hard, with impatience. Kay hadn't realized just how broad, and silent, and empty the library was, or just how softly Will was speaking. Chastened, he took the girls' hands and, taking them around the wheel, led them out of the library.

After the hall, through another low, thick-walled door arch, the five of them came into a corridor, almost a tunnel. This, unlike the library, unlike the tapestried entrance hall, was not at all empty: wraiths were swarming through it, weaving round and past one another—with grace, yes, but also with worry, pace, determination. Some of them, like Foliot and

Firedrake, were frowning, and many of them held papers under their arms. Kay wondered if these were yet more inventories, the lives in catalog of yet more missing fathers or mothers.

Or missing children.

The thought took her guts in a fist and twisted them. In a sudden panic, she nearly collided with Foliot as the two leaders drew up short before a small wooden door. Firedrake raised his fist, hesitated as if listening for something and then rapped twice, hard. The door swung open.

The halls had been magnificent, and the tapestries engrossing, moving. The room into which this squat door opened was completely unlike those. For one thing, it was dark—so dark that it took Kay's eyes a while to adjust to the light as the wraiths, ducking, ushered her and Ell both in. For another, the ceiling was low, and Will had to compensate, partly by leaning over and partly by bending his legs, just to keep his head away from its rough stone surface. But what really made the room unsettling for Kay was that it was filled with short, stumpish wraiths barely taller than herself, and nowhere near as lean or as graceful as Will, or even Foliot and Firedrake. They looked, she decided, positively gnarled, their faces and hands studded with wartlike protuberances, hairy, ruddy and thick-lipped. Fifteen or so of them sat writing at two large trestle tables on either side of the room, and another five or six carried papers back and forth between the tables and a set of large chests lining the walls. At the far end of the room, up a step and behind a magnificently carved desk, sat a single hunched figure, muttering as he angled his head over several piles of papers. His right hand was on the table before him, bunched into a tense fist, so tight that the individual muscles in his fingers stood out in the low light. At the hush that fell over the room, he looked up.

"Ghast," said Will, with a whispered emphasis.

"Gross," murmured Ell, with no emphasis at all.

"At last," barked Ghast, raising and slamming his fist down upon the table with a crack.

For all her bravado, Ell shuddered next to Kay, and her hand went suddenly clammy. Kay squeezed it hard, willing herself to be strong.

"So," Ghast went on as he rose from his chair to tower diminutively behind the desk, "you have really done it this time, you incompetent. I spelled out that inventory in my own hand, you tunnel-scraper, you useless silk-spinning, stone-plotting, muse-loving freak. I should have thrown you out with the poets and that ragtag fantastical scum. And I would have, if it hadn't been a comfort to watch you pulling your guts out of your own backside. You leek, you brainless eel. You're very nearly as incompetent as you are"—he looked Will up and down, then sneered—"long. How could you *possibly* have mangled this assignment any worse?"

Ghast had started forcefully, but he finished with a roar that, Kay thought, seemed beyond the capacity of his stumpish frame. He stopped, apparently to lick his thick dry lips. Will raised his hand as if about to speak.

"Don't say a word." Ghast cut him off. "So these must be the children. Tell me," he said to Will much more quietly, his eyes never leaving the painfully cramped wraith as, with a prowling excitement, he circled round to the front of the desk and stood at the edge of the step. "Tell me, you monster, did you ever in your life think you would again be so privileged as to see, to meet or to remove an *author*?" His every word was a snarl of scorn. Kay stood a little prouder as she felt Will's hand lightly on her shoulder.

"By the muses, no," he said quietly.

"Leave the muses out of it," Ghast snapped, again visibly annoyed. "You know I don't tolerate that kind of talk here." He paused, and the room was silent but for the papers rustling at the tables around them as the little troll-like wraiths went about their work. Occasionally, they snatched furtive glances up at Ghast. "No, you never thought, did you? Never hoped. And now you've gone and plucked her right out of her childhood, right out of her apprenticeship. Poor lamb. Poor fatherless child. It might have been kinder to have strangled her in her bed."

At this Kay started at last. A little cry must have erupted from her, for Will's hand tightened on her shoulder, and Ell was immediately clinging to her left side.

"You know, it does me good to see a great wraith like yourself, one of the old guard, the oldest, playing your part in our little revolution. It warms me. You have even exceeded the little cameo role I allotted you in your own destruction. What a colossally cack-handed klutz you are." Ghast smiled, revealing in his square jaw two rows of sharp yellow teeth. *Like a rat's,* Kay thought. He stepped down off the ledge, lower but somehow, as he approached them, still more commanding with every pace he took. Kay's ears throbbed with rushing blood. "Oh, calm yourselves," he snapped, looking pointedly at the girls. "We're not going to hurt you. Not today, anyway." Kay leaned into Will's hand, but she didn't flinch.

Foliot and Firedrake stepped to the left as Ghast approached, Foliot holding out to his master the crumpled sheets of the inventory. Ghast took them and carefully pried them open, smoothing them with his hand, totally engrossed for what seemed like an eternity. Then, still looking down, he confronted Kay, raised his head and, in a voice so authoritative it was almost silent, said slowly and simply, "The tooth."

In spite of herself, Kay's right hand came out of her pocket and rose into the air, around the tooth that sat upright in her palm. Without taking his eyes off hers or moving his steady face an inch, Ghast took it. Every muscle in Kay's body seemed to rebel; and yet every muscle in her body seemed to do exactly what Ghast demanded.

"Thank you," he said. Sarcasm, not kindness. Wheeling, he strode to one of the long tables, next to which Kay saw the sacks that Flip and Will, Jack and Sprite had lugged back from the balloon, crammed with her father's things. Ghast dropped the tooth into the open fold of the nearest, and then stopped. He did not turn, did not raise his head, but said with the same quiet authority, "I will want to examine this author for myself later. For now take her and—and the other one—to the Quarries, feed them and rest them. Foliot, Firedrake: I will take advice on what to do with them after that. First see these sacks into the cellars. Go."

The two sharp and officious wraiths each hoisted one of the sacks, crossed the room and ducked out through a low door. For a moment there was silence. Ghast had paused by a low mahogany table, his back toward them. His finger absently caressed a stack of papers. He seemed to be lost in thought.

Ell had already retreated to the open door, and was holding on to it like an anchor in a wide sea. Kay felt Will starting to turn her with his still-strong grasp on her shoulder, trying to lead her back out of the room. But Kay struggled free and took a few steps toward Ghast. Her head spun.

"We came here to find our father. Where is he." She didn't ask. She simply blurted.

The same ruffling of papers and soft tread of indifferent feet around the room marked the heartbeats as they rushed in Kay's chest. Ghast said nothing for a long time. She watched his knuckles on the table, still tight, then whitening, as if he were growing angry or, she hoped, afraid. She couldn't see his face, but only the scruff and mat of the tangled hair at the back of his head, and the rough wool collar of his heavy tunic. She waited.

Then Ghast spoke, again quietly; but with the knuckles on the table almost silver now, he spoke with a new, singular menace. "I have already finished with him. You are too late."

No. No. "No!"

Will reached out his long arm and dragged Kay, screaming, from the room.

Ghast paced around the huddled form where it lay on the stone floor of the Imaginary. It was wrapped in dirty cloths, bound with coarse ropes. Only the head was free of them, though it was matted and caked with sweat, and worse. Two squat wraiths huddled to one side, hooded, still muttering and whispering in fervent bursts, maniacal phrases and threats.

"Is he ready?"

One of the wraiths fell silent. He looked up at his master with a pooling, blank stare. In the half-shuttered light his pupils slowly began to acquire focus, as if his gaze were a bird flying in on a tumult of wind from a great way off.

"Nearly."

"He remembers nothing?"

Just at that moment a breaking groan rose from the huddled body on the stones. It contorted, pushing against the cords that bound it. Ghast was reminded of a beautiful moth or butterfly, struggling fruitlessly in its brittle chrysalis. He had seen one once, in a hot season, writhe against its shell until it was exhausted, and died.

The shape lay panting. It groaned again.

"My daughters."

The slight smile drained from Ghast's uneven face.

"He remembers one thing," said the wraith.

"Then work him harder. Give him no rest. The trap is laid. I must have him in the morning, and he must be ready."

"Yes," said the wraith, and turned back to his work, hiding his face in the heavy shadow of his hood.

Ghast watched the scene for several minutes. He was careful not to make a sound, even matching his own breaths to the rise and fall of his servants' rhythmic monodies. Their words were not audible to him, but he knew what they were saying. He had designed the technique himself. Again and again they would regale their victim with lies, with false stories, alternative histories, presenting him with a hall of mirrors in which he could not find himself. Their voices would rise and fall, waxing and waning like the drone of locusts eating away at his peace, eating away at his confidence, finally eating away at everything he knew, or thought he knew. He would fall from an irritation into a trance, from a trance into a frenzy and from a frenzy into a weakness. And in that weakness he would at last relinquish his grip on his own story. He would cease to know himself.

Then he would be ready. When a man reached that state, he was entirely without integrity, without solidity of any kind. He would believe anything, trust anything and, like a man hurtling through a void, would grasp at anything at all as if it were solid ground. To that man, even the slightest dream seemed a hard and reliable fact, every flashing fantasy an eternal reality. He would become so hungry for conviction that he would believe anything, so trusting of everything said or done to him, he would become entirely, utterly untrustworthy. In that state, in the very height of his weakness and vulnerability, they would release him. Just like that. Let him fend for himself then, when he could not. Let him tear himself to pieces in his madness. Let him be mocked by children, kicked by passersby, taken for a vagrant and locked away, or worse.

To think that this was the man who once thought to rebuild Bithynia, that this was the man who aspired to raise the Shuttle Hall! A man! As if a man, just any man, could do such a thing. Even in his most brainsick delusions, surely no man could be so foolish, or so arrogant. For years he had chased Ghast's servants upon the sea and land, harrying them, stealing from them, seeking to seduce them from their service and weaken the wraith who held the mountain.

I hold the mountain.

Ghast smiled. It pleased him to think of the Builder, the great architect of a doomed hope, staggering through the streets of some unfamiliar place, pursued by children and lunatics.

Once, you hunted us, thought Ghast to himself, as he turned and stalked from the room. But now they will hunt you.

5

The Quarries

Afterward Kay could not clearly remember what happened next; she seemed to float through more corridors, tethered listlessly to the others. Sounds—voices, footfalls, the opening and closing of heavy doors—reached her only distantly, as if they were smothered in cotton in an adjacent room. She would recall a sense of downward movement, as if they had descended a long incline. Sometimes other wraiths, both short and tall, passed them in pairs or small groups, less often alone. Though tethered securely to her sister's little, fierce hand, she felt numb and cold and empty; her bones seemed to have drained within her, and were shuddering like hollowed canes in her legs. She had so many questions, and no strength to ask them.

Dad.

A few times, as they swept ever downward, she faltered. Each time Will's hand was there to catch her, to prop her up—as if he had read her mind, as if he knew the ache and emptiness within. At first she was grateful, but then she became irritated. She wanted to fall. She wanted to collapse—but he wouldn't let her. He seemed to be on her side somehow, but more and more she felt in his gentle support the arm of a jailer.

And then they seemed to swoop through a low arch and into another gloriously cavernous and entirely vacant womb of a hall. This one, unlike the first two, was not at all furnished or lit; but it was much, much bigger. Across the distant ceiling—if it *was* a ceiling—as the girls craned their necks in wonder, they saw tiny points of light like stars, swirling and cascading in patterns far denser and more ordered than those of the constellations. The soft light they created illuminated very little of what was around them, except to give a general sense of gloomy, cavernous waste. On the cave floor Kay could see nothing in particular at first, but from a number of directions she could hear water moving, as if there were a stream nearby; and a fresh and constant breeze stirred her hair.

Will turned, crouching down to talk to them.

Ell prevented him.

"Is this a dungeon?" she asked.

Forthright and uncowed, like Dad always says.

"No," Will answered her. He reached out to tousle her hair, and then thought better of it. "We're in the Quarries. It's not much, but this is where we live. Where the wraiths live, I mean. It's an unspoken rule that we don't speak in the Quarries—well, it *would* be unspoken, wouldn't it?" He smiled. "Here we are wordless, though in your case I think anyone would make an exception. Still, try to keep your voices down. I'll show you where you can sleep."

Taking the girls by the hand again, Will led them farther down, this time by a short, steep flight of steps into what felt at first like a pit. When they hit the bottom of the steps and turned through a gash in the wall, they found themselves in another room with a kind of window to one side. A partial ceiling of broken arches left voids open above to the roof of the cave. Lanterns were hung here and there. Exhausted, Kay slumped to the floor, cradling Ell on her lap. Will pushed a heavy wooden door shut behind them, put his hand to the key in the lock, then hesitated—and, thinking better of it, left it alone. From the table he took a dark loaf of bread, broke it and handed two wedges to the girls. It was the sort of rough, dry thing that, normally, they both would have refused. But now they ate hungrily. As Kay chewed, the sound of water, louder here, came to her ears.

"Are we near a river?" she asked.

"Yes, we are, of sorts," said Will, now taking a stone jug and pouring some water into small clay beakers that he handed to the girls. "You're drinking it. When we were delving here, centuries ago, we exposed one of the old currents from the glacial melt to the east, tunneling here through the soft stone of the mountain's lower buttress. We dug it out and quarried around it, which left us with a very useful water supply and a continuous source of beautiful music. This may not be our true home, but it has its consolations."

"And the stars?" Kay asked, pointing weakly up.

"We cut shafts directly up through the mountain there to the sunlight. The shafts help to circulate the air, and they are, you have to admit, spectacular." He smiled broadly. "It was my idea."

Kay thought wearily that it must be day. *How was it day. What were they doing. Where were they.* So many questions started in her exhausted heart, she couldn't keep track of them; she felt them sputtering in her throat like wet candles.

"Since coming back into the mountain, we do everything here but our work."

Kay opened her mouth and a confusion of half-formed questions seemed to emerge at once. "Your work?—but why did you come back?—what is the mountain?"

Will nodded once, then pulled over a small table, along with two chairs that had been left by the wall. He put each of the girls on a chair, and sat on the floor, facing them.

"It's simple, really. Wraiths tell tales. Wraiths remember tales, write tales down, conserve them, circulate them. Wraiths *are* tales. As you saw, our library is one of our sacred and most important places; there we keep written copies in hundreds of languages of all the tales that ever were, are, or might be. We study them, copy them, preserve them, and travel the world listening, whispering, singing. Tales quicken the imagination, and excite the mind to dream; but they also rely on logic and reason, and anyone who tells a tale must be a master of narratives. We came to the mountain to hide—from a world grown suspicious of stories, a world that has forgotten where truth really resides."

Kay tried to focus. She leaned away into the hard struts of the straight-backed wooden chair, pressing her bones against the ridges. She rubbed them painfully from side to side as she looked about the room, willing herself to be alert, to pay attention. Everywhere she looked, she found distraction. In some places the room had been chiseled out of the rock, in others practically gouged. Across the ceiling and floor, the rough strokes of the hammers were sometimes still visible, the surfaces left unfinished, creating dips and rises everywhere. But around the window and the door that stood opposite the gap through which they had come in, it was different. Here with fine tools some workman had carved every edge precisely, patiently cutting out figures in the stone, pillars and fluting; and, though there was no system to it—it seemed to be a haphazard collage—it was beautiful, like opening the door of an old wardrobe, Kay thought, and finding it crammed to bursting with a snowy forest. Now that her eyes had grown accustomed to the low light, she realized that the stone was not exactly the dull gray of granite but a faint blue, like the sky in the east the moment before dusk. Looking at it, she let herself be lost in it.

"Why did you quarry here? Where is all *this*?" she asked, lifting her left hand again and gesturing around to the huge void left by the quarried rock. The limp sweep of her hand took in the room and the huge expanse of the room beyond the door.

The door Will had almost locked. Had he intended to lock someone out? Or was he about to lock them *in*?

Will frowned quickly at her question, and clasped his arms around his knees, digging in his chin. "All this stone is in Bithynia now," he said, his voice almost as hollow, almost as faint, as an echo. His eyes closed, and Kay could tell, as she had on the balloon, that more was coming, if only she would wait. "Here in the Quarries we carved the sky-stone, then floated it down the river to the sea. There, on the coasts of Bithynia, we built. From the mine below the mountain we dug out gold and silver, rich veins with which we threaded the living wood of our halls. Now the Quarries are our home, and the mines—"

But Ell cut in: "What did he mean, that . . . loud man, when he said he had 'finished with him'? Is our dad here?"

Will opened his eyes but did not look up. They were wet with tears. At first Kay wondered if the sorrow was for his home; but then suddenly she felt she knew why he had thought to lock the door, why she had lost her interest in questions. She willed him to stop, not to say the words. Not in front of Ell. She wanted to stand up, to lean over, to clap her hands over his mouth. But instead she sat frozen, the high back of the chair cleaving into the back of her skull.

"No. He isn't here," Will started, his voice rising—but then he stopped. With a finger of his right hand he followed the ridges of the textured floor of the cave, their ups and downs, their starts and stops, their half-moons and careening circles. Kay watched this movement closely, aware that its expressive patterning, like the movement of the stones on the plotting board, was rich with significance. Then the finger began to lift, and was soon tapping out random points across the floor, as if mapping raindrops or pecking for grain. "No," Will said quietly, his tone softer, "no, he isn't here."

"Then where is he?"

Still uncowed.

The finger went on tapping, tapping. Kay watched it for a while, then looked over at her sister. Although Ell sat a head lower than her on the next chair, her expression was so alert, her eyes so wide and her strawberry hair so electric with her absorption that Kay felt as if she herself were instead looking up at her sister.

"After removal," Will said quietly, "there is dispersal."

"What does that mean?" Ell asked, not missing a beat. She swiveled toward Kay. "I don't know what that means."

Will was silent, but his finger still plucked and dived,

though it was slowing. Kay wanted to reach out to Ell: she understood enough of what "dispersal" meant to know that it sounded bad, horrible, wrong. Too much like "disposal." But Ell was still strong and resolute in her defiance.

Will looked up and unfurled his hands over the floor, palms down, as if warming them on the creases and hollows of its rough pattern. "Let me tell you a story," he said.

The little girl shot back, "I don't want a story. I want to find our dad." She did not even flinch.

"Still, this is a story that is about finding. Sometimes there are truths and comforts and ways *inside* stories that are not so apparent *outside* stories. Sometimes stories are answers, or make answers possible. Sometimes they are the mothers of answers." He was staring hard at Kay now, directly into her eyes. When she met his gaze, she thought his eyes were the calmest, most ice-like blue she had ever seen. She felt as if tears might well out of her fingertips.

"Many hundreds of years ago, before histories were written down in books, great cities and nations told stories about themselves as a way of remembering who they were, where they had come from and what they wanted for themselves and their children. The men and women who told these stories were poets, and because they had to remember huge numbers of facts—names, places, events, in a web of causes and consequences spanning hundreds, even thousands, of years—they had to come up with ways of making their memories stronger. More secure. So they fashioned their stories into rhythms and rhymes, lines and verses, and decorated them with distinctive patterns of language that would help them to put every piece of every story in exactly the right place every time they told it. And they told their stories often: every night, sometimes to one or two children, sometimes to crowds gathered around a great fire or under the stars on a summer evening, they remembered, and they witnessed, and they prophesied."

As Will spoke and his finger wove across the stone, Kay felt his tone change, and change again. It was like looking through a kaleidoscope, where the colors and shapes shift as it turns, building patterns as delicate as a butterfly's wings. She heard kindness and compassion, brilliance and vision, and beneath it all a music she was sure she knew: the music of her father's voice, reading, reading, reading in the dark of the night. Ell held out her hand and Kay took it; somehow they managed to slip to the floor, and sat clasped together in the shadow of Will's voice, two children poised on the brink of sleep.

"Now, turning your story in just such a way that it was most beautiful, most striking, most memorable was a great skill and a gift—something that could be learned, but only by those who were born with a readiness to it. And so famous families of poets arose, men and women with that readiness, who were trained in the mysteries of speaking and who conserved the traditions of the nations, and the cities, and the families. And they competed with one another; some were considered lesser, others better, and some very few the best.

"Among the best—by far the most celebrated, and indeed the greatest—was the poet Orpheus. He was born the only son of a long line of singers, and the talent ran so rife in him it was said that he himself would never have children, that he gave so much to his tellings, he had nothing left to beget. Stories must be his children. Everywhere he went, he went singing; his fingers danced in the air, plucking notes from the breezes, or from the rain, or from shafts of light that dropped at morning and evening between the clouds. As an infant, before even he learned to speak, he learned the rhythms and tones of the ancient modes and melodies, and they were constantly in his throat."

"Was his father proud of him?" asked Ell. Kay glanced sharply across, annoyed at her for breaking the flow of the tale, annoyed at herself for being annoyed. Ell was sleepy. Her eyelids were sinking.

"Yes, very proud," said Will. "For he quickly mastered all the traditional tales on which his father's reputation had been founded. He sang the great battle stories, with their interludes of love, and the fortunes of the famous dynasties descended from the heroes and the gods. As a young man, he was already capable of a depth and range of narrative, memory and passion usually reached by only the best singers in their prime. It had become a speculation on everyone's lips: Where would this great artist go next? Where would he find his material? It was the custom in those days for poets to rely on certain tricks of the memory to make the delivery of their songs easier—certain elements of a song would resurface again and again, like bells ringing: four- or five-word phrases, sometimes slightly altered but still roughly the same, returning to the verse like a refrain. This made the poet's load lighter, but also delighted the audience: there is nothing more satisfying than the return of something familiar. There is nothing like ease in the midst of difficulty, nothing like cool water at the height of a hot day. Orpheus, beyond all the other poets of his age, had become adept at this technique, and was famed for the subtle ways in which he could lay down a theme or a motif, let it change or vary, and then lie fallow before reviving it, calling it back into the light. Where other poets would make in their poems a web of themes, some of which they caught up again, and others not, it was said that Orpheus never lost a single word. It was said that he could let a word die and go to hell, but he would ransom it back again before the poem was done."

Kay bristled. *Go to hell*, she thought.

Ell hadn't drifted off. "No one comes back from hell," she said.

Will's finger stopped in the air, and he raised his head to look at the girls, each in turn, for a long moment. His eyes seemed full of care for them, as if they were small and helpless. "Should I keep going?" he asked.

Kay nodded. Will's finger began to move and move. It took him almost a minute to join his voice to it again.

"It was maybe inevitable that so skilled and able a craftsman should fall in love with the Bride. She never comes freely to those who love her. She must be sought, though never directly. One day her lovers find her as they go about their trade. So did Orpheus as he sang beneath a spreading plane tree in a valley in Macedonia. He had been reciting one of the older tales—a history of the making of the world. The best stories pose impossible questions: If a creator makes all of creation, where is the creation that made this creator? How could he make the world, and yet be made, too, by that making? As Orpheus sang, he began to lose control of his song. Instead, it started to take a purpose and a length of its own. Story after story ribboned from his aching tongue. Searching for one thing, for one great story, he made many. It was far into the night when, in a mood created by his exhaustion and the accelerating rhythm of his invention, he began to see something new, something dazzling. In a voice of sudden thunder he threw it from him like a bolt: the very impossibility of the world was its cause. This is the greatest mystery of the Bride.

"That night, through a copse at the edge of the village, Orpheus glimpsed the Bride for the first time. She wore the same loose-fitting white gown as always, the garment that had first given her her name. She moved silently and at the edge of his vision between the trees. The Bride never appears except, as it were, in a shadow or a reflection; you can no more look directly upon her than you can upon the sun. She can be seen in other things, through other things, as if she were a light on the water, or the sudden hues hanging in the air after a storm. Orpheus could feel this, could feel that he must not turn his eyes directly upon her; and as he looked away with the song running through his mind and his ears, her white gown drifted ever toward him until he could feel her breath weaving through the hair on the back of his neck. He thought then that, if he lost her, and the touch he knew she was about to bestow, he would never be able to invite her presence again. He was wrong. It was only his first time."

The Bride of Bithynia, Kay thought. Her mind ran to her father's study at St. Nick's, to that foot stuck in the door. "The Bride," she said. "Who is she? My father works on her."

Will's finger kept moving, this time dancing over the stone like a feather floating on water. "No one knows who she is," he said softly.

"But Orpheus *saw* her. You said he saw her. So what does she look like? Who is she?"

"She is that thing that no one can ever see clearly. The thing you can almost grasp, the thing you can very nearly make out, but then it eludes you—she is what gets away, like a thought or a vision at the moment you start from sleep, like the strand you lose when you gaze at the twine. Or when you love someone very, very much, and you think you might almost burst—she is the bursting."

"Oh, oh, oh," Kay cried, as if she would weep, even though she knew that her heart and her head were clear and dry. "He can never see her."

"Never," agreed Will.

"I can't stand it," said Kay, tightening her arms around Ell, whose warm, huddled body had sagged into sleep.

"He couldn't stand it, either. The song ended for Orpheus that night, and he did lose the Bride; but only for a time. Another time he again took up his lyre, and sang, and she came to him. She came again and again. He became so practiced at invoking her presence that soon he had only to slip into that familiar mode of thinking or telling, and he would catch sight of her white shift, or hear the light step of her sandals on the grass behind him. It was never the same thoughts, of course—a thought is like the track of a cart-wheel in the dirt of a road: the more you think it, the more you run it down the road, the more it sinks in, becoming a rut; and a rut, growing muddy, chokes the passage, and that is fatal to the rhythm of the Bride. Always, therefore, Orpheus sought out new stories, new rhythms, new modes in which his thought might tumble over itself, like a wave endlessly reverberating against a shore but never breaking; so that he might live every day in the expectation of a presence, the sense of companionship and witness that he had never before had occasion to feel.

"What the poet had not counted upon, but what others saw in him from the start, was the way this hunger for the Bride was changing him. He was gradually being torn apart from within. As he searched tirelessly for more experiences, more stories, more rhythms, more forms, always after a new means by which he might summon the beautiful, fugitive figure that was almost within his reach, it was true that his art soared, and that he became the greatest poet of all the ages. But his innovations and experimentations, his long nights without sleep and days without rest, the months after months when he stood chanting ever new, ever more complex and moving tales—all this came at a price. The love of the Bride gouged him, scooped at him, quarried him. His eyes sank in his head and his lips paled and cracked; his hair came loose and was shed; his muscles dwindled and his skin grew sallow; his tongue dried; and in his temper and thought, too, he grew more brittle, less resilient. Finally, one day, coming out of the mountains of Thessalia and taking a seat in a crowded market to tell a variation on the most ancient narrative of the flood, the inevitable occurred. Orpheus's rhythm had become so strong that the Bride, rather than stalking silently behind him, appeared to be running toward him from far off. And as he sang, the faces expectant and full of delight around him, at last he looked up, full into her face as she approached. And at that moment, slowing, she reached out her arm and touched him."

In the long afterlight cast by the starry holes in the roof of the cave, Will looked slowly down at the faces of the two girls, now slumped against each other, arm in arm, on the ground beside him, the regular, almost silent rise and fall of their breaths indicating how fast asleep they had fallen. He drew with his finger absently on the rock of the cave floor, tracing ellipses.

"Will?"

Kay was awake again and murmuring, though her eyelids remained slack and shut, and her arms limp where they draped round Ell's shoulders.

"What happened when she touched him?"

Will drew a single full breath. By the time he let it out, he wasn't sure if Kay had drifted off again. She wasn't sure, either. "He came apart, Kay. And he was dispersed."

"Bring him."

The two hooded wraiths approached the crumpled form, one on either side, stooped, and with the utmost gentleness, lifted it to its broken height. The man's head lolled on its neck, spluttering through the filth of mucus and blood that caked its face. Whoever he was, now, he did not look up. He was ready.

Ghast held wide the oak door to the Imaginary as the wraiths guided the shuffling form between them, and together the four of them descended the sloping stairs of the tower. Their progress was painfully slow.

At the base of the tower Ghast put his hand on the heavy rope and collar from where, for centuries, they had hung on an iron hook. How often had he imagined lifting it, in waking visions as in his dreams! The collar was plain iron, a band of about two inches in width, hammered flat, with a tight hinge to one side and a clasp opposite. The clasp was mounted with a heavy ring, long ago welded to its base with huge slugs of black iron. He knew before he touched it what its weight would be, how its hinge would demand forcing. Beg for it. The inch-thick rope had been twined with a thread of steel, then spliced to the ring and the rope ends woven seamlessly back upon the cabling. He drew it slowly from the hook, allowing its mass and heft to shift slowly, coil by coil, into his other palm, each coil a distinct pleasure. To each filament he gave his thumb, but delicately, noticing every ridge and hair as it slipped with its own weight between his hands. It would end too soon, he thought.

It ended too soon.

The head hung before him, its spare remaining tufts of hair clotted with filth. He had no inclination to touch it. He nodded to one of the wraiths, who grasped the hair firmly, lifting the head far enough to expose a band of gray flesh beneath the chin. Ghast broke open the collar with a single sharp tug, then placed it around the figure's neck, as lightly and reverently as if he were crowning a king. And in a way, he was. Though the reverence was for himself.

As the little group moved through the rough-quarried passages, Ghast always leading, the rope pinched tenderly between the tips of his squat fingers, he thought of the great triumphs of an earlier age, of the generals returning to the imperial city in chariots crowned with golden victories, of the captives paraded in chains, or cages, through the jeering tumults of the streets. He imagined the trumpets, the velvet cushions on which the emperor, seated, would receive with gracious condescension the submission of his enemies. Courtiers lapped up his yawns as cats do milk. With every step he felt their drums pulse up his dwarf calves. He did not need to close his eyes; the vision settled on him waking.

With no haste they entered first the great cavern of the mountain, hung with tapestries, then by a little passage, the door to the library. The lights flared along the walls as Ghast shuffled his prisoner in behind him.

There he and the wasted figure stood. They were ready. The only thing left to do now was wait.

Spiders wait in their webs, but neither, he thought, as patiently nor as silently as he. Soon his daughters would see the great Builder; but the Builder would not see his daughters. For he no longer knew them. To what desperation and recklessness this would drive his enemies Ghast needed not imagine—for his servants had plotted every step of it already. The girl would break. After that she would do anything to get her father back. And when she learned that only Ghast himself had that power, why, she would give him anything he demanded. She would give him a golden crown.

Until then, he would wait.

6

Dispersal

Kay woke to hands on her shoulders. *Why?* she thought in the moments before she forced her eyes open.

It was Will. He was crouched above her, arguing with Flip. Kay saw his mouth moving, and understood the metallic clang of his angry tone, understood the hard clamp of his eyes, like a vise, as he volleyed words over her head. But, still dull with sleep, she couldn't make out the meaning.

And he was holding her shoulders. She pushed against his hands, writhing in his grip against the stone beneath her. Somehow they were up on the floor of the quarry, in the large space, and there was movement—she struggled onto one side, thrashing beneath Will's strong hold—and she saw a knot of wraiths moving away across the quarry floor and toward the great stairs.

"I don't care about the thread," Will was saying. "He doesn't have the right." He was hardly paying attention to her as she pushed against him with all her strength.

Ell, she thought. Her eyes rebounded wildly around the huge space, her head lurching from side to side. *Ell. Ell.*

"Right or no right, Will, for the time being he has the voices, and there's nothing you can do about it. We have to make the best of what we can. Don't get too involved with this." That was Flip.

Where is Eloise?

"She's only a tiny child. She can't be more than six years old."

"She's eight," Kay corrected him. It came out like a howl.

Now, at last, she had Will's full attention. She pushed hard to the right, then rolled immediately to the left. Will's right hand slipped, and Kay sprang onto one foot. She kept low in a crouch, like a dog. A wounded one. About a meter away. She watched Will's hands.

"Where is she?" she said. "I promised I would stay with her."

"Foliot came and took her to see Ghast," said Will. "I tried to stop him, but my *friend* Flip here stopped me." He was steady, and kind, and like always. *But his hands. He was holding my shoulders.* "We thought you might wake up," he added, almost apologetic. "And the way we plotted things, we were afraid you might try to run after her."

Kay glanced quickly at that knot of wraiths still moving across the floor of the Quarries, now very close to the stairs.

"You mean Ghast wanted to see her?" Kay asked. "I thought Ghast wanted to see *me.* Take me there now." She didn't move. The wraiths didn't move. They said nothing, but she could sense from their intense silence that there was going to be a problem. The wraiths on the other side of the quarry floor reached the stairs, and began to ascend out of sight. In among them as they climbed, Kay caught the flash of Ell's red curls.

Then she was gone.

Her whole body flinched.

"We can't leave, Kay. Ghast's orders," Will said finally, softly, and Kay crouched on the ground again, her hands pressed palm down on either side of her, and looked out into the distance, to the other side of the quarry, beyond the stream where it gushed up from below. There were other wraiths coming and going here and there, silently in the shadow. "The truth is," Will said, "they want me to lock you up."

"No, the truth is," said Flip, "he wants me to lock you *both* up."

Kay ignored them. "But what does Ghast want her for?"

"I don't know," Will said.

Kay turned. "She's scared. I promised I would stay with her."

For a long time they just watched one another—or, rather, watched the spaces in between one another. Around them shadows flitted in and among the rocks, and soft footfalls echoed from the tunnels that led out from the cave, so distant and muted that they reminded Kay of the sound of stones settling in the silt of the river when, the summer before, she had gone swimming underwater with her father. Her dispersed father. Ell had been throwing stones from the bank, and Kay had watched them plummet down, making the lightest thud as they half dropped, half settled into the weedy mud. She had decided at the time, as she held her breath and squinted through the murky water, that it was the sound of fairies stamping. She hadn't been far off, she now thought with grim satisfaction; it was the sound of wraiths walking. Kay felt a stiff and brittle rage steel through her shoulders: it was the sound of wraiths walking off with Ell, she thought, while she slept, while Will did nothing. While her mother, alone at home, cried.

Kay stood up. "Well, I don't care. I'm going to Ghast. You're going to have to stop me."

She was off and running before they could react. This gave her a few seconds to get ahead. She ducked behind a cleft, darted up through a narrow channel in the rock, then doubled back down some stairs, through one of the quarry pits. They couldn't have seen her go down, she knew, because she was light and low, and had had enough of a start; and at the bottom of the stairs she waited to see if one or both of them would chance it—but they seemed to have gone in the other direction, toward the tunnels. She was now too far down to see them, but there was a glow where the tunnels opened up into the cave, and so she headed in the opposite direction, picking her way as quietly as she could and always looking out for other wraiths. She was hoping that there would be another exit, some way to slip past Will and Flip, get to Ghast and . . . well, at least be with Ell. Even if she couldn't get her out, at least she wouldn't be alone.

Kay found herself at the low, sudden bank of the

underground river. It flowed here silently, a bluish-gray column of glass laid in its cut bed like a massive dark jewel. Kay stood watching its apparent motionlessness, looking for some sign—debris, an eddy, a bubble—of its current, knowing that it must be motive and fluid. Mesmerized by its stillness, she crouched down and gingerly stretched out her hand to dip her fingers into the water. The moment of contact came as a shock: it was liquid ice, not water, and from the dead force of it against her fingers she knew that it was moving very fast. After a few seconds, her fingers already numb, she withdrew them and stood up. She backed off and reminded herself of what her mother would say: *If it's that cold on your fingers, Katharine, you certainly don't want to fall in.* Kay smiled; *no, I certainly do not.*

But with the tingling that was beginning in her hand as the cold leached out of her fingers came a thought. She spun round to face upstream, training her eyes along the embankment as far as she could see in the dim light. There was a curve in the course, slightly up and to the right, and some outcroppings that blocked her view; but she thought she could just make out, not too far away, that other tunnel out of the Quarries, a tunnel that had not been carved by wraiths, but scoured by the cold hands of the swift-running river.

If there is water flowing through this cave, it has to come from somewhere.

She ran along the bank, grateful to the wraiths for having left a path clear all the way to the wall. Flip and Will would assume she would be running for the quarry entrance; instead, she made for the river tunnel.

By the time she reached the gushing, noisy mouth of the stream, she was breathing hard, and had to stop to get her bearings. No one was following her, though it could surely be only a matter of moments before one of them plotted her escape, before one of them saw her hovering. She peered into the dark mouth of the underground watercourse, where it cut upward through soft rock. The wraiths had obviously dug out the channel for some way into the mountainside—but how far? If she went in, would she be able to get out? Kay thought: *The wraiths would probably only have taken the trouble to cut the stream's tunnel open if they were using it for something. It goes somewhere. You don't delve a dead end directly into a mountain.*

Do you?

The sound of what she thought might be footsteps disrupted her thoughts. She didn't look back; she sprinted into the dark.

In the thick chill of the black tunnel she soon found she had to grope her way along, using her hands against the wall to guide her, and running her toes along the wall, too, with every step. She was terrified of putting a foot wrong and tumbling into the stream to her left. For a moment she stopped completely, too anxious to move forward, too reluctant to turn back. But the thought of Ell alone with Ghast drew her onward again. And someone must be following by now. They would figure it out. They would have lights. She had to keep going.

Kay forced herself to make progress—slow progress up a slight incline, but progress. She felt the air growing cooler and cooler as she bored further and further into the mountainside.

In the darkness Kay suddenly recalled those final words of Will's last story, which she had heard just before drifting off. *He was dispersed,* he had said. Orpheus, the poet, had been dispersed. Kay remembered the myth of Orpheus's death, a story her father had told her a hundred times if he had told her once: how he had descended to Hades to redeem his dead wife, Eurydice; how he had lost her; and how, while singing his songs of lamentation and despair, he had been attacked by frenzied worshippers of the god Bacchus and literally torn to pieces.

Dispersed. So this, then, was what Ghast had meant when he said it was too late.

In the dark of the tunnel, her arms splayed on the gently sloping rock face, Kay suddenly felt sick, disoriented, vulnerable—and she nearly reeled backward. It was as if someone had just turned on a very bright, high-beam light right in her face—except that, instead of a light, it was darkness itself they were shining upon her; high-beam darkness, totally unilluminating her. She crouched. After removal, dispersal. And now they had taken Ell. *Why? What do they want her for?* She had to keep going.

By the time Kay found herself alongside a warm and suddenly very dry section of rock, she was so tired with her fear that she almost failed to notice it. A realization was only just settling in her mind as her hands brushed up against a new texture, one that was definitely neither dry nor wet rock. It felt like wood; and at the center of it there was a metal knob or handle. The blood in Kay's arms and legs flushed into her chest and neck, and she came up square against the door, the silent river running on behind her. Feeling round the frame of the door, she could tell she was going to have to push. So terrified and exhausted had she become that she hardly paused to wonder what might be on the other side; she just pushed with all her strength.

Nothing happened. She pushed again. Nothing. Her whole head a throbbing mass of despair, she almost cried, and pounded with her fist on the wood.

Finally, the door swung open with surprising force, and Kay tumbled into what seemed a blindingly bright room. Her eyes seared by the change in the light, she was able to take in only that the room around her was warm and cluttered, though it was as silent as the passage she had left. It was only then she realized: she had fallen into someone's arms, and the sleeves and coat up against her face were similarly warm, and smelled strongly of some spice she couldn't precisely place—not mint, but as sharp; not aniseed, but as sweet. Another form—a black blur—had rushed across her to close the door as she fell, and she felt the draft settle as it closed and then—it sounded—locked behind her. For a long moment nothing else happened, and she remained immobile, semiprostrate, her head buried in the cloth of some stranger's arms. Then he spoke.

"It's all right, Kay. I've got you. You'll be fine."

It was Will's voice: unmistakably soft, almost a whisper,

with that delicate unsureness that made his assurances so believable. She let herself go limp. *But those hands.*

"Will, they're coming."

Kay stiffened a little again. It was Flip. She pushed herself up and tried to open her eyes. "How did you find me?" she asked. "I need to find Ell."

"This will do for both," said Will, taking something out of his pocket and thrusting it into her hand. It was a small, smooth, cool stone. A plotting stone. "We plotted your run just now, and we can plot Ghast, too." Will smiled weakly and held up his hands. *Those hands.* "It's our one advantage on Ghast—and we reckon we've got about thirty seconds till we lose it. Get up—quickly now."

Will's arms were around Kay, hauling her up, and then he and Flip practically lifted her in the air as, together, they drew back into the near corner of the small room, behind two tables stacked high with carpets, to rest beside an enormous trunk. To her left, she could see the door through which she had come in. It was flush and seamless with the wall except for a handle which, judging from its shape and size, was exactly like the one on the other side. She could now see that the handle was in the shape of a plotting stone—oblong, smooth and jet-black—but larger.

But to her right . . . To her right, she suddenly realized there was only gloomy air. Over a rail, a kind of balcony, her eye soared out into a chaos of shadows.

"Into the trunk," said Flip. "Hurry."

From a pocket Will produced a ring of keys, holding them up to the light just long enough for Kay to see how similar they were to some she had seen before—where?—and then, selecting one, he undid three separate locks on the battered, banded trunk. When its heavy lid swung open, Kay could see that the blackened interior was almost empty, and easily large enough to fit them all. But, helping her in, Will quickly let the lid fall over just the two of them, keeping it propped open ever so slightly. Through a crack Kay could make out Flip, still outside, striding away, the cloth of his cloak whispering urgently as his long legs made for the opposite side of the room. Away to the right, lights suddenly flared, and she realized that beyond the railing, below and all around, was the great library of the mountain through which they had walked the night before. Everywhere around them were shelves crammed with books, and Kay saw that they were in an alcove perched just above the hall. She shuddered, for no reason that she knew.

Flip bent rigidly over a table; just to his right was a stack of papers, which he was making a show of reading.

"Will . . ." Kay whispered in the dark within the trunk. Her breath rebounded hot against the tight space where they crouched. "What are we waiting for?"

"We're pretty sure Ghast is coming. And he will have Ell with him, or will know where she is. We figured it out on the plotting board."

"And that's how you found me?" Kay asked. She recalled, in the Quarries, looking over toward the entrance of the tunnels, and glimpsing a group of wraiths gathering around the light. No wonder they hadn't been searching for her, she thought—or, rather, they *had* been searching for her in their own way. They had just been looking for where she *would be*, rather than where she *was*.

"Yes," Will said.

"But . . ." Kay paused. "Then why can't Ghast use the plotting board to find the two of us?"

Will's reply was immediate. "Ghast and most of his trusted servants are hopeless with plotting boards. They can't use them well. Anyway, your path through the Quarries was unusual, random, unpredictable. That kind of chaotic improvisation makes plotting difficult for anyone but the best." She could almost feel him winking in the darkness. "If Ghast tried to plot this now, he would probably think we were still down there."

"Why can't we just use the plotting board to find out what Ghast is doing with Ell? Why can't we use it to get her back?"

"Too much, too far in advance. A plotting board is excellent for predicting movement, but poor on intentions. It can give us a good idea of where someone will be, especially soon, but it doesn't tell us a lot about what they mean to do. So I was pretty sure—I knew—you would be on the other side of that door, but I didn't know how you would feel about seeing us."

It was almost like an apology. Or it was an apology. In the trunk Kay took Will's hand and squeezed it. Will seemed almost embarrassed.

"And I am pretty sure Ghast will be here, in the library, in a few seconds. So we wait."

That's not right.

Something about Will's plotting was off. Kay felt its wrongness in the back of her mind, the way you notice, without really knowing how you know, that a picture hanging on the wall is askew.

"No," Kay said. The word just flooded out of her. "No, that's wrong."

"What is?"

"We're not waiting for him. *He's* waiting for *us*." All over her head Kay's hair pricked and stood up, like a wave sweeping back from her eyes, across her scalp and down her neck. In her mind, she backed away from herself.

"Kay, what are you—"

"I think I dreamed this."

There was just enough light in the trunk for Kay to see Will staring at her, to see his mouth opening in puzzlement—but just then a loud, low hiss came from across the room. Kay's eye shot back up to the crack to find that Flip hadn't moved—he was still hunched over, one arm laid loosely on his pile of papers, apparently hard at work.

"It's time, Kay," Will said. "Stay absolutely still."

There was an abrupt and sharp noise, as of a latch being lifted, that echoed through the library. A confused number of footsteps, heavy and light, sounded around the vast space. Kay could make out very little, save for the dim suggestion of forms moving down below.

Flip was now on his feet.

"It's you." That, she knew with conviction, was Ghast's voice calling. She hadn't forgotten his scornful, raspy bass.

From the edge of the stone balustrade Flip looked down, his silver hair catching the light. "I'm going through the receipts of dispersals, Sergeant Ghast, as you instructed at our return yesterday. So far everything seems to be in order."

"I trust you dispatched the papers for the criminal More this morning?"

From below Kay heard the sound of metal scraping on stone, and a low, moaning sort of grunt. She pushed at the heavy lid of the trunk with her shoulder, widening the crack, and tried to peer below to the right of Flip's leg. Try as she might, she couldn't get an angle—all she could make out was the warty crown of Ghast's head.

"Well?" The head hardly moved, but the voice had hardened in anger.

"I did as I was ordered," came Flip's curt reply.

"Such a pity you had to lie to the girl. Well, weave the thread, weave the thread," Ghast said, his tone heavy with sarcasm. "Foliot will attend to his unraveling. For now, I have another dispersal to enroll. Firedrake."

Firedrake passed in front of Ghast. His long, limber form

towered over his master, and Kay had for a moment a clear view of his sharp, set features. Before—when they had first arrived at the mountain—she had thought him officious; but now he looked mean, his face harder and more evil than any other she had ever seen. *Remember this,* she told herself. *Whatever happens, he is an enemy—an enemy to anything good.*

Flip looked to his left as Firedrake's footsteps sounded on the tight circular stairs that led up from the library floor. Kay shifted again in the trunk, propping the lid open a little further than before. She felt Will's hand grasp and squeeze her shoulder, though he didn't dare speak. But she would not hold back.

"I think you will find this dispersal, too, has been duly registered," Ghast said.

Firedrake was now only a few meters away. He stopped. Nothing happened.

"May I ask by what authority this thread is to be cut?" Flip had not taken the piece of paper. It didn't look as if he had even acknowledged Firedrake; instead, his hands were firmly planted on the stone ledge before him. "As Clerk of Dispersals, I usually expect notification and the customary consultation period before a formal consent can be taken."

Ghast's reply was immediate, as if he had been waiting for

this objection. His tone was suddenly almost jocular. "Oh, read it. Read it—it will amuse you. I wrote it myself."

Firedrake stepped forward and handed the piece of paper to Flip. "Read it aloud," Ghast said. "It will give me pleasure."

Flip took a deep breath and began.

"Sergeant Ghast, Steward Controller of the House of Bithynia, Master Extraordinary of the Weave and Chief Clerk of the Bindery, to all wraiths and phantasms, greeting. Whereas it has ever been our confirmed power to act summarily in cases of exceptional danger to the Honorable Society, whether present or forecast; and whereas such summary power has been severally exercised in times past by three of our immediate predecessors in the office of Steward Controller, outside the normal course of the thread; and whereas the Steward Controller is bound by oath to defend the Honorable Society from perils present and to come by oath and by duty, regardless of interest or consequence; remembering always both the responsibility of and respect for the office—"

"What is he saying?" whispered Kay to Will. "I don't understand. Is someone else being dispersed?"

Will didn't answer. He only gripped her shoulder, hard, and didn't let go. Kay could see in the near darkness that he was straining after every word. Bewildering as it was, she groped after the sense as Flip kept reading.

And then she heard it.

"—it is now our grave and careful responsibility to command the summary dispersal of Eloise Worth-More, author, daughter of the silkrunner and enemy of the Honorable Society, Edward More, who is called the Builder. Her thread will within these twelve nights be measured, cut and undone, and its several remains littered in the corners of the earth. By me this twenty-fifth day, etc."

It was all Kay could do to stop herself from screaming as Flip finished intoning the words in a dispassionate, clerk-like voice. Her chest tightened like a limpet on a rock, and her head surged.

Ell. No. No. Let me. Let me go in her place—

"On what grounds do you invoke the summary power of the office?" Flip asked.

But I am the author. Let me—

His hand still on her shoulder, Will pulled Kay gently back as she struggled against the lid of the trunk. She knew she would prove no match for his strength.

"The little girl is an author," Ghast spat. "You know I am no friend to authors; in their frenzies and raptures they think themselves gods, and their innovations are a threat to the order of the thread. A threat I have stamped out. Besides, she is the daughter of our greatest enemy these two thousand years. The mere coincidence of danger and power is enough to license my action. Firedrake will carry out the dispersal. You and your disgraced friend will see that the older child is disposed of. She may see this and that, but she is worth nothing. I do not greatly care where you lose her."

Despair. Anger. Fear. Sorrow. Shock. Disgust. Bitterness. Confusion. Kay sank against the floor of the trunk. *Nothing. Worth nothing.*

She didn't know what to think, or how she felt. The pain in her coiled body seemed to be a kind of cavern into which she could cram them all. As she started again to stand up—just as the tension and tightness began to flex in her legs—Will gripped her shoulders with both hands. *Those hands, always holding me back.* He hardly moved, and she realized that he must have been waiting for this, waiting for her to try to explode. *Always holding me back.*

"Not now," he whispered—so low, so close, that no one could have heard them. Even Firedrake, not three meters away. "Trust me. You can't do anything for her if he finds you."

Flip had still said nothing. Kay watched his back, willing him to shout, to defy Ghast, to do anything, to do something.

Firedrake went down the stairs. Below, where Ghast stood with his acolytes, there was no sound.

Don't accept it, Kay thought. *Throw it all back in his face. Tear it up.*

"I will enroll the dispersal," said Flip.

No. "No," she whispered. "No. No. No." Thick sobs surged up from her chest, and she choked them back as best she could, whispering "No" to every tear that ran down her cheek.

"Firedrake. The staff."

From her place beneath the lid of the chest Kay saw Firedrake hand Ghast what looked like a long metal rod—the height of a tall man at least, and clearly heavy. Moving stiffly, Ghast seemed to insert it into a hole in the floor, so that it stood erect. He stepped back and paused, regarding it, then placed his hands securely on it, palm over palm, and bowed his head briefly in a gesture that suggested prayer.

"Your little trinket," he called out to Flip. He was beaming. "We haven't used this contraption in some time, have we." It wasn't a question.

"It's the great wheel," Will whispered. He was choking out

the words in a strangled whisper, his heart twisted in a tense struggle between outrage and fear. "He's going to turn the great wheel. Kay, he won't dare—it's sacred . . ." The urgency of Will's whispering simply dissipated, like lingering leaves blasted away by a gale.

Ghast was straining against the rod, pushing it. With an enormous effort he seemed to shift it to the right. A rasp as that of metal on stone filled the library, and then a sharp rap or clack echoed its report as the rod settled. Ghast pushed again, and with great effort shifted the rod, turning something on the floor until it slotted into place with a shudder.

"There," said Ghast. He turned to face Flip, lifting his face in a leer and opening his arms as if in welcome, or in triumph. "It's a pity," he called out, "that we no longer hold our little twelve-night festival, don't you think? A pity that we no longer turn the wheel. Perhaps we should. Perhaps, just this once, we will make an exception. A new kind of festival. One night of the twelve is already gone. But see that this dispersal is properly enrolled, and, on the twelfth night, let it be performed. We will have our festival again. A festival of dispersal!"

Ghast was almost laughing now, but even from afar Kay

could see how the big distorted laughter on his face only thinly disguised the bitter scorn of his heart.

Down the stairs, the door to the library suddenly opened again. Kay heard footsteps.

"Ah," said Ghast with a simpler and more cheerful brio. "Foliot. And our little friend."

He must have turned. Again, Kay pushed at the lid of the trunk, which creaked slightly as she wedged it open. She now had an unimpeded view of the little group in the center of the library, in among the long, lighted tables. Two hooded figures, one tall and the other very small, then Firedrake, Ghast—and, on the floor beside Ghast, a huge bundle of rags or cloths. What was that?

"Greet your daughter, silkrunner," said Ghast, and he hauled with both fists on a rope.

The bundle of rags jerked into life. It raised its head. It said nothing. Kay's breaths became shallow; all words fled her grasp.

And she knew.

Kay stared at the head, willing it to turn toward her, willing it to recognize her. And then, as if by a kind of magic, it did: slowly the chin turned on the neck, and the face lifted, and the blank eyes met hers, and she knew that—even concealed, at such a distance, in the trunk, through the railing—those eyes *saw* her. And yet they did not know her.

Then there was a scream. The room screamed. It went on and on. It deafened her, split her, cut her ears and cleft her heart like an ax. Kay felt herself juddering, felt the trunk juddering with her, felt Will rising, enclosing her huddled and broken form in his arms. *Still those hands.*

Her father. That pile of rags. Her father. Those hands. Her sister. Her father.

My father.

The scream, Ell's scream, went on. Within its awful clamor no one could hear Kay's own sobs, no one noticed the commotion of her spasms or the gentle ministrations of the soothing wraith who held her, whispering to her, "We will save her. We will save her. I will save her. My dear child, we will save her. We will do everything."

With her head buried, sobbing into Will's chest, Kay didn't see Ell being dragged out of the library. All she heard was the rising, hysterical notes fade as the door was shut upon them, and they disappeared entirely. Kay shook still, but silently. Will clasped her as tightly as he could, all pretense of concealment gone. But Ghast wasn't looking up any longer. They were safe.

"That," said the voice she hated, "was very satisfactory. Firedrake, see to this dog. And you, Philip," said Ghast without looking up even as he left the room, "take care of the other child. Perhaps a cliff would be convenient. I will have more orders for you before long."

Kay started to rise, throwing aside the lid of the trunk with the careless force of her desperation. Flip thrust out his palm, flat to the ground: *Stop,* it said.

But she wouldn't. She stood. She closed her eyes, inclined her head, opened them again—and watched as Firedrake dragged her father from the room by a rope. He scrabbled along the floor like a dog, repeatedly falling to one side, then lurching up again as the wraith jerked at his collar. Had Flip not covered her mouth with his hand, she would have called out to him, or cried, or screamed, or all at once.

The far door closed behind Firedrake. Kay slumped to the floor.

For a long time all three of them sat in silence. Kay kept her eyes closed. She concentrated on her breathing and tried to allow all the other thoughts to fall away, or to settle in the steady rise and fall of her chest. It was hard to let them go: again and again they reared and pinched her—her father, her sister—and again and again she let the thoughts fall. At last she opened her eyes.

The others were looking at her. Their eyes were steady, their faces kind.

"So," she said, "is that dispersal? Is what they did to him dispersal? Why would they *do* that to him? What do they want with him? What has he done to them?"

"Yes," said Flip. "Dispersal. That's how it begins."

"And what is this place?"

"It's the Dispersals Room, where the records of all removals and dispersals are kept. Since Ghast took over, we've been recording here a sort of unofficial history of the great creative minds in human history."

"You mean the most creative people always get removed and dispersed? Like Orpheus?" Kay was silent for a moment. "Is that why Ghast—my father—because he's *clever*? I don't understand; why do you *do* this?"

"It doesn't make much sense to me, either," Will replied. "A long time ago, in another life, I was Chief Clerk of the Bindery—the office you saw yesterday, where Ghast's flunkies write their records and reports and their orders and—well, whatever they write nowadays. But when I was Chief Clerk, things were different. In those days we only removed real criminals; the kind of people whose stories might actually hurt someone." He sighed. "Or a lot of people sometimes. But in those days we hardly ever went so far as dispersal. It's much better just to put them in the mines—"

"Will."

"The mines?" Kay felt suddenly alert, again on edge.

"The river," Will said, hobbled by Flip's warning. He gestured toward the rear door, the door through which Kay had come in. "It goes down—where we mined for metals and gems—in the mountain."

"It's a kind of prison," finished Flip. "Only for the worst. Real criminals—not just Ghast's enemies."

"And my sister?" Kay said. She couldn't even say it. *The author. Ell. The author, Eloise Worth-More.*

"Probably," answered Flip. He couldn't say it, either. "Will, we were wrong—about the—Did you hear him?"

"I heard him," Will said. "I don't know what to say."

I'm not worthless.

Kay looked from one face to the other, knowing that both

wraiths were evenly balanced between a desire to explain everything and a need to keep her ignorant. This was a balance with which she was growing ever more frustrated. She held her head as high as she could.

"I know I'm not one of you. I know I'm a child. I know I'm not my father." She looked hard at them, willing them to see her seriousness, her sharpness, her weight and determination. She tried to pinch a furrow in her forehead. "But you have to tell me what's going on. I heard Ghast say that Ell is an author, like me. You have to tell me what all this means. Don't lie to me. Don't try to hold me back. I need to know how to stop Ell from being dispersed. I heard Ghast say it. Twelve nights. I need to get to her." *Time is running out.* The image of her father's crumpled, twisted body flashed through her mind. *I'm not going to let*—that—*happen to her.*

Flip stared hard at Will, who was about to speak. He stopped. Flip took over.

"An author is someone born with the ability to receive the highest skills in narrative; it's not a power, but a readiness to acquire a power. An author is the kind of person who somehow already knows all the stories there are—as if they don't even have to make them up, but just remember them. It is rare:

neither Will nor I have seen an author in a great many years. Not a real one. This doesn't mean that they don't exist—it's just that we don't always know where they are. They must exist; they always have. We were authors once." Flip paused, looking into Kay's eyes almost bashfully, apologizing. "Not every author becomes a wraith, but all wraiths were once authors. And with plotting boards we can find new authors—we can help them, enable them, teach them, foster them—but only if we have time, a lot of time. And there are so many people in the world, and so much to plot: we'd need centuries to search a single country. More often, in the past, they just appeared, as if by chance; and if we knew about them, it was only after they'd passed away. Sometimes great authors don't become known as such until centuries after their deaths. And so we don't get to them in time." Flip stopped.

"And these days," Will added, "ever since Ghast more or less declared war on authors, it's better if we don't find them. To be honest, if I'd seen the last page of the inventory we were given, I'm not sure I ever would have gone to your house at all. To remove a child!" Will buried his face in his elegant hands.

"We thought—on the inventory it said that the daughter of

Edward More was an author. We thought it was you, because you could—see us."

"But we were wrong," Will said from within his hands, not daring to look at her. "It was Eloise."

Kay suddenly realized that she had been surviving on little more than a hopeful sort of self-importance. Now she felt her expectation collapse like a flimsy box crumpling under the heel of Ghast's boot. His words rang in her head. "She is worth nothing." "I do not greatly care where you lose her." "Perhaps a cliff would be convenient."

I was never an author at all. All along it was only her. How foolish I was. How vain. How typical.

She gasped for breath, and stared at the oversize plotting stone that was the handle of the room's rear door. "So you," she said, "you were authors, and now you're you." Her hands, normally so expressive, dangled limply at her sides. "If I'm *not* an author, then what am I?"

Will brightened. "You—you're just something we haven't quite figured out yet."

"But how can I help her if I—if I can't—if I'm not—" Kay simply came to a stop. Her face was blank.

"You can if I come with you," Will said.

"Will. Not a good idea." Flip sat down suddenly at the large table, as if he had just been handed an enormous and insupportable weight. "Earlier, outside, I heard Ghast and Foliot talking about more than just a dispersal. They're going to summon a Weave on Twelfth Night. I don't know what he's playing at. You need to be here."

Will didn't hesitate. "There's no point in my being here, Weave or no Weave. I feel like I lost the thread a long time ago, and I'm not going to get it back now, Flip—you know it as well as I. If I can do some good here, then, by the muses, I'm going. Let Ghast summon his Weave. Someone has to take a stand against him."

"What do you mean? What's a Weave, and who will come to it?" asked Kay.

Flip lowered his head onto the tips of his fingers—not, Kay thought, in despair, but in intense concentration. One hand, coming free, danced a little in the air, the fingers picking out rhythms and depths while the head, still bowed, rested motionless. Kay knew he was plotting. Why wouldn't anyone answer her?

"What is it? What do you see?" Will dragged a chair next to him. "We need a board."

"No," said Flip, looking up, dazed. "It's something else. Something isn't right. It's as if we were working with the wrong information, as if Ghast were lying—but about what?" He was talking to himself, in a kind of reverie, and the words floated past Kay, almost incomprehensible. "I can't understand why he would disperse this author. And why put it off till Twelfth Night, when we all know—when this Weave is so important. And that gimmick with the wheel—How dare he! He's *got* to be playing at something."

"The Weave is a grand assembly of all wraiths and phantasms," Will said, interpreting for Kay, his own fingers now beginning to dance across the table and chair where he sat. "So, everyone will come—all the wraiths there are. We only call them in extraordinary circumstances; for instance, when the Honorable Society is changing officers. When we're under attack. Or when, as legend has it, we crown a king. Which we have never, ever done. Which is why it's only a legend."

"So, Ghast wants to be king?" At first Kay was dumbfounded. But something was niggling at her just as, hours after waking, a half-remembered dream flashes through the mind and is gone, and flashes again, too fast to be handled. "That's why he took Eloise," she said. She didn't know why she said it.

Will looked at her sharply.

"Maybe," Flip said. "That may well be right. Legend tells us that the crown must be placed upon his head by an author; not by a wraith who was once an author, but by an author. Most of the wraiths still take these matters seriously, and this little detail has kept Ghast in his place for some time." Flip looked ashen. "But he may at last have found his opportunity; which is why we're amazed that he would squander it so recklessly, dispersing the very means by which he might at last satisfy his ambition. It doesn't add up, doesn't plot right. A king is sovereign, uncontrollable, beyond the law. A king can act outside the Weave. A king can abandon the thread altogether. He himself becomes the thread. It is him; he it. And if that's what he wants, if he really wants to be king, your sister should be just what he has been looking for for quite some time."

Will was watching Kay intently. It made her uncomfortable. Flip was easier. He continued to rock his head up and down, his fingers tapping it and circling in tight patterns around his ears.

And then, all of a sudden, he slapped his hands down on the table before him, startling them both. "I just can't see it, Will," he said—hard, impatient. Kay had never seen him like this, and maybe Will hadn't, either. "There's something wrong with our plotting, but I can't figure out what it is. We're going to need help if we're going to stop this."

Will spoke quietly, never taking his eyes from Kay. "Are you saying you're in, Flip? Are you saying you'll fight this?"

Flip suddenly looked up at Kay. His eyes were as hard and as black as a plotting stone. "As Clerk of Dispersals I had to let them do it—take your father, your sister. I had to stand here, in this room, and seal the order, and watch them go through those doors down there. There was nothing I could do."

Kay stared at him. Hard.

"I am ashamed to say it. I didn't know until—Anyway, I did what I had to do. And now they are both gone."

Kay's eyes slipped out of focus and she couldn't wrestle them back. "Gone." *Why?*

"If I had refused, some other wraith would have been chosen in my place. Some other wraith would have done it anyway. Some other wraith would sit where I sit now, and I would be under guard in the mines."

"Maybe," said Kay, hot with anger, "that would have been a better place for you."

"No," said Will. "Flip is a friend."

"Then he should start acting like one," Kay spat.

Flip sighed. "In a way, you're right," he said. "We've been trying to keep Ghast close, to watch him. You can't plot a stone you don't hold. But maybe we've gone too far. Maybe we've been too ready for too long to do Ghast's bidding." Flip inclined his head to Will, and Kay saw that his eyes were not black at all, but marbled with green and silver. Everything softened. "She's right, Will," he said. "This is no place for us anymore. The best place for us—for all three of us—is anywhere on the move. There *is* something wrong with my plotting; I can't figure with a free hand anymore. Every time we do anything, it seems like Ghast has anticipated us. It doesn't make sense; everyone knows he's not a good plotter. And yet he knows."

Flip stood up abruptly, knocking his stool with a clatter against the wall. In a few paces he was at the rear door and had taken the heavy stone in his hand.

"Kay, you were right. We have to run, and we'll have to be sudden. Unpredictable. Spontaneous. Impulsive."

With a heave he threw open the door, and the room flooded with freezing, dank, mossy air.

"Are we going down to the mines?"

"No," said Will. "That he would expect. We'll never save

her that way. Never let someone else plot you like a stone—not even Ghast. Maybe he thinks love makes us simple, easy to predict. Foolish. Maybe he thinks it makes us vulnerable."

"It does," said Kay, doubtful. *And why shouldn't it?* Her heart and thoughts tore to the mines, and she longed to let her feet follow. She fought down the thought of Ell screaming, kicking, frightened; or scared, sullen, locked up in the dark and cold. She would gladly give herself up to hold her sister, to promise her anything—

"Love keeps its promises," said Will. He held his hand out to Kay, and she stood. "Love that moves mountains, love that flies through the air, love that dares to imagine anything. I promise you we will save your sister. But right now we have to run."

"Up," said Flip as they swept through the door, turned right and began to climb through the darkness. "By the air, through the air."

"The fox always runs to his den at last."

Ghast leafed absentmindedly through the papers stacked on his desk. He had no time now to sit down and deal properly with the hundreds of reports, proposals and analyses that his Bindery clerks had prepared for him. A few of them still toiled in the old business, collecting myths and histories, stories, poems, tales and fables—the eternal process of conserving all that is told. There were still a few scouts and wispers who roamed the world beyond the mountain, and from time to time returned bearing trunks filled with papers and scrolls and books of all sizes. These materials had to be enrolled, and copies lodged in the library. Yes, a few clerks still worked on these old tasks; but he had reassigned the rest to his own new project. This was still something of a secret, even in the mountain, for most wraiths would not yet be ready to surrender their plotting stones, or to shut up the doors of the Imaginary forever. But that day was coming. There would be no more need for plotting, or for imagining, when his Bindery clerks had finished their analysis. Very soon he would have an algorithm to create any sort of story he wanted.

For now, it all looked in order. It would be. Fear was a great motivator, and his servants well knew what was in the mines.

Ghast surveyed the Bindery. Twenty-three junior left-wraiths, all as squat and sour-faced as he, hunched over their low tables, writing. To his left stood Foliot, one of the old guard to be sure, but submissive. Ghast declared, to no one in particular, "Their love will make them careless." No one dared to acknowledge his words, though all had heard. He loved to speak to them in this way. To speak to no one at all.

As he crossed the threshold into his private closet, he motioned impatiently for Foliot to remain outside. Ghast closed the door and began to change into his traveling clothes. For many years he had covered and disguised himself carefully whenever he left the mountain—which was not often. One took precautions when one was being hunted, especially by imaginers. Especially by the oldest, most cunning imaginer of them all. Now the imaginers had been driven from the mountain, and dared not show their faces. His fear was less. Now he could walk freely, and he intended to cut an ostentatious figure equal to his status.

He would never be king in the mountain. His adversaries underestimated his reach. He would be king in Bithynia, or no king at all. He would not just win the battle. He would not just win the war. He preferred not to destroy but to compel his enemies. They would serve him, even in the sacred precincts of their own temple.

And what could a dog and its two delirious pups do about that?

7

The Thread

Outside the Dispersals Room Flip's flashlight punched a hole in the darkness. Kay could see well in both directions—downstream from where, an hour before, she had blindly groped her way up the tunnel from the Quarries, and upstream along the steeply winding course of the underground river. The water rushed gray and glassily by, about four feet below the ledge, which she could now see was broad, and continued to run along the stream as it rose upward. Will was moving his hands in the air, his distant gaze absorbed with plotting.

"How far does this path carry on?" Kay asked.

Will's hands stopped midwhirl, and he looked directly at

her. "The tunnel goes all the way to the top of the mountain. I think we should take it."

Flip, who like Kay had been waiting on Will, looked sharply at his friend. His face was all criticism, concern, caution. Kay thought for a moment how much he was like a parent, and Will the child. "It will be much faster to go through the Quarries and down the mountain. Going down, we can run. Going up will take hours of climbing—hours we don't have."

"I know. But, like you said before, there's something wrong with this whole situation. I don't know what it is, either. I can't quite tease it out; but one thing is for certain—they'll be waiting for us in the Quarries." Flip raised his eyebrows to an almost comical height that his light only exaggerated. "No," Will said. "The Quarries are the safe option. If we're going to escape from the mountain, we need to do it with daring. Let's go for the cliffs."

Perhaps a cliff would be convenient. Kay was sure she didn't want to run into Ghast or those two skinny predators, his servants Foliot and Firedrake. *But.*

"Say we make it," said Kay, spinning round. "Say we make it out of the mountain. Where do we go from there?"

"We go home," said Flip. "Your home. Will, we—"

"No," said Will. "We keep going. We need help. Nothing scares Ghast now."

"One thing scares him," said Kay. She was absolutely sure of it, as sure as anything. The claim poured out of her with a conviction that frightened her, because she had no idea where it came from, or why she was so certain of it. "Imaginers scare him. We need an imaginer."

"Yes!" cried Will. "When plotting doesn't work: imagining!" Immediately he set off to the right, up the steep slope alongside the black glass of the silent water.

In the light of his lantern Flip raised his eyebrows and pursed his lips in disapproval. For a long moment he stood like this, then shrugged and motioned for her to follow. Kay felt like shrugging, too.

What followed felt like hours of climbing. The walls of the tunnel gradually closed in around them, and the air grew drier and colder. The passage narrowed and then, without warning, it ended.

Will had stopped just ahead in the gloom. He knelt on one knee and ran his open hands across the floor of the tunnel as if over still water.

"Hundreds of years ago," he said, an intense look of

concentration on his face, "we came to these mountains to quarry their stone. To build our halls. We took it down into Bithynia along the river—down the very same river that had first led us here, up from the fertile valleys and through the foothills to the west. When the river went underground, we followed it, because we had seen in its waters the telltale mineral traces that we knew came from the soft, carvable stone we craved for building. We delved most of this path through the mountain for transport, as far as the Quarries, and further. But this section—the part we have just climbed—was different."

At that, Will came bolt upright and seemed to tug at something. Kay could see the glint of metal in his hands; it looked like a huge brass ring.

Flip carried on. "When the barbarians drove us from Bithynia, we had nowhere to go but here. No one knew these caves like we did; and few knew them at all, or even how to find them. We came up the river, taking only what we needed for our stories: the boards and stones, the books and the tapestries. The great wheel. Our tools we had left here long before, and in time we had transformed this shelled-out waste of caverns into—"

"Not much more than a shelled-out waste of caverns," said

Will, looking up in disgust from the floor, where he continued to heave back on the brass ring.

"In any case, we came here. At first we expected them to chase us daily—the warring tribes, rapacious and violent men and women who had neither time nor love for stories. They drove us from Bithynia with fire and sword, and with fire and sword we feared they would follow us. When they didn't come, we thought they were preparing a siege. We did a lot, then, to make this a fortress, and self-sufficient, but we always knew we might need a way out. Something remote, something unexpected. And that's when we built this part of the tunnel up through the mountain—right here to the very steepest part of its peak. We call it the Needle. From here, we might escape in time of crisis. As it happened, our pursuers never came, and we never used the tunnel."

Will looked up abruptly, and with a grim and pained look on his face said suddenly, "Back—move back."

Kay and Flip shuffled back down the tunnel as fast as they could, watching Will struggle to his feet with a long chain in his hands, taut as he dragged it with a sort of shuddering, raspy groan from the floor. A sudden tremendous rumble filled the tunnel, and Kay had only a moment to turn before an explosion of gravel and dust shot toward them, pelting then engulfing her. The dust stung her eyes like wasps, and she felt her throat seizing, choking. She held her hands to her face, crying and screaming—and would have gone on trying to scream had Flip not doused her head with water, then firmly pushed her down toward the floor where the air was blissfully clear. She gulped breaths.

"What—what was that?" she begged him, inches away, in a whimper. "What *happened*?"

"With any luck, if the floor held," answered Flip, "that's our way out of here."

At that moment Kay realized that, riding on the cloud of dust and noise, there was light, floods of it, and it only grew now that the dust had begun to recede. She and Flip crawled along the floor, taking meter after meter with agonizing care, until their hands reached what felt like a hole in the tunnel floor. Air rushed past in a crisp wind.

Kay dared to pull her head over the edge and look down—

And might have screamed again—had the view not sucked the breath from her lungs. Under the floor was nothing at all: a vast, dizzying void of empty air, yawning for hundreds of meters along a sheer cliff face down to the rocks below.

Perhaps a cliff would be convenient. I do not greatly care where you lose her.

Kay froze.

Flip put his hand gently on her shoulder, and then—*mercy*—drew her back onto the solid rock. "For these last few meters the tunnel is at the top of the cliff, inside a large, single piece of stone jutting out over the valley below. We needed a door that no one would ever find from the outside. The sky *is* above us; but it's also below us. And so there was a real risk that the floor would collapse when Will opened the door." He smiled. "But we didn't fall."

Kay laid her head on the grit, pebble and stone of the floor and closed her eyes. Her head swam. For the space of a breath, she thought she couldn't do it, couldn't go on. But then she put before her mind the image of her little sister, impulsive, fierce, loving, vulnerable. Eloise.

I will dare anything to find you. Twelve nights, Ell. He's given me twelve nights to find you, and twelve nights only.

It took them almost an hour to climb down the hidden handholds that, hundreds of years before, had been driven into the cliff face. Will had gone ahead, but Flip guided Kay's every step from just below, easing her feet slowly down the face of the sheer mountain's side. It was still morning, and though the air was warming, the wind jagged and gusted at them from the north, cold on Kay's ankles; eventually her hands, too, became so chill that she could barely grasp the freezing iron bars. A single glance below her, though, was all she needed to renew her resolve.

"Now, Kay, jump!"

Only three meters or so remained when she leaped free of the rock face and collapsed heavily into the two wraiths' open arms. Firm ground had never been so sure, and she found herself sobbing onto the cracked brown stone where they had finally landed. The tears dropped down her cheeks—like climbers falling from the mountain, she thought—and smashed on the pebbles beneath her. One after another, in their dozens or maybe hundreds, they splashed into oblivion, barely staining the hard earth where they fell.

"Welcome to the Eagle's Nest," said Will. "I'll check for company."

Kay followed him with her eyes as he vaulted onto a ledge just beside them, then scrabbled into a carved niche—a concealed perch from which he could command a view not only of all to the north, but over the ridge to the mountains south and west of them, too. This vantage point had been hidden even during their descent. Before Flip could stop her, Kay had leaped up the ledge to join Will.

"Kay—no—you don't—"

But it was too late. She dug her fingers hard into Will's sleeve to steel herself as the panorama wheeled below her and she wheeled above it. The openness made her feel sick, as if she were somehow flying, high, without wings.

"Don't look down," Will murmured. There was something fierce, settled in his voice.

Kay shuddered. Far off she could see endless blue, hard and unremitting sun, metals glinting in the sand-colored mountains, snow. And below was the river. Its soundless, turbulent current tumbled from the mountain just opposite their perch, then snaked down a steep valley and curved in and out of sight miles away, until it disappeared at the base of a massive hunch of distant stone.

"There are wispers abroad," Will said quietly, and he pointed to the left, then straight ahead, where up on a slope Kay could see a tiny black form descending. "Ghast's scouts. Centuries ago they were rangers and pilgrims, the kind you read about in all the old stories, who roamed the world collecting tales, gathering poems, making records of all the new myths and song cycles. In times gone by they used to bring them back to Bithynia for the library. But now they're just common spies working for Ghast. Most of them can hardly tell a joke now, let alone spin a yarn. They've lost the thread."

"Tell me about the thread," Kay said. "You keep talking about it."

"Tell yourself about it," said Will, gesturing out to the mountains before them. He instantly realized that he had sounded curt, rude, dismissive. "No, I really mean it. Look at what's in front of you. I think you'll understand."

He hunched down to mark the wispers. Kay looked out from between two stones. In all the mountains and low hills that stood before her she saw nothing but rock and low scrub. The rock lay brown, in places reddish under the glare of the noon sun, and the scrub looked winter-beaten and dry. It patched and clumped on the slopes as if huddling against the wind and cold. Everywhere the cold had left its marks—not just in small lingering fields of snow on higher and sheltered ground, but in the stains on the cliffs, on the tumbling scree of loose stones and rubble that she knew had been broken and cast down the mountain slopes by ice, freezing and thawing, then freezing again over the years.

What does he mean, tell myself? What does all this emptiness have to do with threads?

The landscape before her was entirely uniform, bland almost. Nothing stood out. But for one thing—the river. *Threads.* She watched it from the point where it issued from the rocks of the mountain, pooled, and then flowed downward, uncoiling among the low slopes.

"It's the river."

"Yes," Will answered over his shoulder. "Tell me what you see. Tell me what the river does."

Kay stared at it, and saw its bends and turns—like the joints of a long, impossible arm. The more carefully she looked, the more tiny bends and turns she discovered in its course. *It turns at every moment. Of course. Every moment is a turn in the flow of water. Every moment of flow is like a choice. It keeps choosing the best way.* "It finds the shortest way down," she said. *The thread.* She thought of her mother, back when she was younger, before all the arguments, sitting at the table with a needle in her hand, picking out its course through the threads of a piece of cloth. "The cloth has its way," she would say. "The cloth sews the needle, and not the needle the cloth."

"The water finds its own way, the best way," Will agreed, as if he had read her thoughts. Or she his. "It goes the way it always has."

"That's the thread, then," said Kay. "It's the way things work best, the shortest and the easiest way, the way things have always been, the channel they cut, the way things smooth out in time, always growing simpler, growing more definite, straighter, easier. It's the way everyone does it together."

"Complexity and change can be beautiful," said Will, "but, like the river in the mountains, they can sometimes be dangerous. There is sometimes white water. Over time, things settle. The river falls into the hills, then into the low plains. It slows down. So it is with the order of things, generally: ideas, habits, customs—they all come into being over time, become regular, become simpler, become easier to understand. That's one reason why we honor tradition together, and that's why we prefer to do some things the way we're *expected* to do them. It's a comfort, and it's simple. That's the thread."

Will went back to observing the wispers, plotting their

patterns as they swept across the mountains, looking for a moment when he, Flip and Kay might break free unobserved.

But Kay suddenly had no interest in the wispers. Instead her eyes were riveted to the river opposite, and to a barge that was floating—so slowly, so far away below—down its smoother lower waters. From her height it seemed tiny, but she knew that was only the distance, that it was a huge thing, and it seemed to be swarming with wraiths. She tried to count, and reached something like fifty.

"What is that? What are they doing?" she asked.

Flip had climbed up to the lookout to join them. "They're leaving the mountain," he answered. His voice was almost a whisper, barely audible over the wind. Kay looked hard at him. He seemed shocked. "They're taking the river out of the mountain. They're taking to the water, for Bithynia."

At one end of the barge—its stern—Kay could see a sort of raised area where there was no movement, no scurrying or hurrying forms. But perhaps there was a chair, or several chairs, and at the highest point—

"Ghast is leaving the mountain on a throne," said Will—to neither of them, and to both of them.

"And what is that building at the front?" Kay asked. She

was mesmerized by the barge's slow, meandering motion down the silent river, by the rhythmic flow of bodies moving across its deck—rowing or punting their way, perhaps fending off the unseen rocks.

"That's not a building," said Flip. "It's a cage."

When Kay cried out, her shrill and piercing voice shattered the silence of the mountains like the call of a hawk. The wispers walking on the mountains below knew how to track great birds by their cries; tracking the screams of a girl, a girl they were looking for at that, and to a place they all knew well, was surely too easy.

Before Kay understood what they were doing, Flip and Will were carrying her down the ledge onto the little platform where they had landed earlier. Then Flip seemed to vault over another low ledge, and disappeared from view. Following after, as Will practically dragged her behind him, Kay could see Flip half leaping, half running down a huge sweep of boulders and scree toward the north and east, away from the river, down to a far, narrow plain at the mountain's base.

Kay dug her heels into one of the rocks and stiffened her legs against Will's yanking arm.

"No," she said. She said it as firmly and as loudly as she could.

Will rounded on her from below. She expected to see anger in his face, or impatience; but she found only kindness, and compassion.

"I'm going down the other slope," she said. "I'm following that barge."

"I am going to tell you something you already know," Will said. He was speaking almost at a yell, to throw his voice over the blistering gusts of the north wind. "Something you don't want to hear. You can't do anything for them right now. Not one thing. All you can do is join them in that cage. Or worse."

Kay wanted to cry, but all her tears had already fallen. She yanked her hand loose from Will's and stood facing him for a long moment. The wind buffeted her trousers around her ankles and seared her dry cheeks. She knew he was right. She knew that the courageous thing to do was follow him, and bend, and trust. *Every bone in my body wants to be on that barge.*

"Down there"—he gestured with his thumb over his shoulder, talking fast—"Flip has a plane. It's little, but it's solid. He says he hates it, but he's a brilliant pilot. And it's the only plane on the mountain."

She gave Will her hand again.

He reached out a long arm and hoisted her body quick as a

flash over the ledge. His eyes never left off scanning the slopes around them.

"You can see them, Kay—the wispers, running."

Kay could see them, from the north and the south, from the west slopes of the two flat hills before them, running. Their paths would converge on the little plain toward which Flip had been loping only moments before.

Will held her by the shoulders and took her gaze in his, boring deep into her eyes. "We have to get to Flip before the wispers do, or they'll trap us all. And if they do, I can't protect you," he said. "And if I can't protect you, you can't save your sister."

Or Dad.

"Or your father."

They ran down the mountain, hurling themselves from boulder to boulder like dancers on a stage, like bees drunk on flowers in the height of summer—barely touching the ground, always looking for the next step, always pitching forward. In what seemed mere seconds they had reached the plain, and Kay ran behind Will, flagging, losing him, over the dusty, weed-choked flat earth. In the corners of her vision she was sure she could see black shapes moving, but she didn't dare look. She just ran.

Kay barely had time to dodge as Flip drove the little plane bouncing from behind a big boulder. He circled, and Kay heard the propeller start to drone as he opened the throttle into the gust swelling toward him.

"Climb in," said Will. "Fast." He wasn't looking at her. He was looking past her, intently. Kay knew what that meant.

She needed no prompting. Down the opposite slope a dark-robed wisper was vaulting over the last stones that separated him from the valley floor. It would only be a matter of seconds before he reached the plane.

With Will's help Kay clambered on to the wing, grabbed a handhold and slung herself over the edge of the rear seat. Flip piloted along the level ground, faster and faster.

Will wasn't in yet. The plane was gathering speed, bumping but starting to race forward. Kay pushed herself low into the warm cushion of the seat, wedging her feet against the wall before her. There was a strap, and she was fumbling with it as a hand suddenly appeared to the side—above her—grappling.

"Flip!" shouted Will. "Let me climb—"

"No time!" shouted Flip from up ahead, pushing the throttle yet further. "We have visitors!"

The plane lurched and bumped over the rough ground for

what seemed like an hour. Kay grabbed at the straps, forcing herself into them. Against the air rushing at them from the propeller, from their own forward thrust, Will strove with every tendon and sinew of his body. Kay watched in agony as an elbow, a shoulder, then his head appeared. His cheeks and lips were deformed by the rushing wind, and for a moment, as he heaved, he looked like a grotesque, terrifying gargoyle on some ancient chapel. Then he sprawled head over heels into the seat on top of Kay, crushing her even as she snapped tight the buckle of her harness.

Finally, the plane took flight, and suddenly, sickeningly, the jolting stopped.

Will's face seemed to be buried in her shoulder. The plane climbed impossibly fast into the sun-shattered sky.

"That went well, I think," he said.

The journey west would take ten days. Three of these they would pass in the high, rocky mountains, exposed to sun and cold gales. Three days they would pass in the high marshes, hidden from the wind by the singing reeds. And three days they would pass in the fertile low valleys of Bithynia, each one lusher than the last, until finally they dropped into the steeply wooded gorge where the wraiths' great hall still stood.

Waiting for its king.

On that last day the barge would rest at the eastern gate. For a wraith who would be king there was but one way to enter the hall at Bithynia, and that was by the Ring. This circuit of the walls, which ascended from the eastern gate by an imperceptible grade to the raised plateau on which the hall stood, was adorned with carved tablets depicting the twelve sources of all story. He knew them as he knew his own face. Every wraith did. Soon he would have them chiseled away.

It was said that that old hag they called the Bride had herself taught the earliest wraiths of the twelve sources. As if she were more than a story herself! In any case, the age of miracles was over, and the Bride, if she had ever existed, was gone for good. No, the guild of wraiths was restless for a leader. A strong leader. One who might give them a sense of purpose again.

Ghast smiled at the smooth current of the course lying between him and the great hall. His preparations had been precise. What is more, his old adversaries—they could hardly still be called that—had underestimated him. They had measured his cunning by their own. It had never occurred to them that he might desire their escape, that he might provoke their hasty flight, that he might have predicted even that which seemed unpredictable—because it was. So heavily did his warts hang upon his cheeks that his deepening smile had the effect of turning down the corners of his mouth. It hardly mattered if the mirror did not find his joy handsome. His satisfaction was his alone, anyway.

He looked with pride at the empty cage where it stood before him on the barge. Set beneath it, just out of sight, was the heavy, forged iron plate of the great wheel. That empty cage, that ancient timepiece—these were better witnesses of his beauty, or his cunning mastery. How he would savor the reports of his wispers, when at length they reached him in the night: how the stones had tumbled from the Needle at the top of the mountain; how the wraiths and the girl had climbed down with labored caution; how the patient wispers had, as instructed, circled the quarry without closing on them; how the fugitives had watched from the Eagle's Nest, then scrambled suddenly down to the valley and taken their feeble little plane; how they took off and flew south. How they thought themselves heroes.

But only he truly knew where they were going. Only he knew what it was all for.

8

PHANTASTES

Kay woke out of nothing. She hadn't known she was dozing, hadn't noticed falling into it, or even being drowsy. Now it was warm and dark. And loud. She was surprised at the warmth, and then, cracking open her eyes in pain, at the sun all around her. The wind rushed by. In her ears she could feel the plane losing altitude; they would be landing soon. She shuffled herself up a bit and pushed one of the folds of the heavy blanket off to one side. Will, who had been watching intently out of the other side, saw her hand move and waved with a smile, then looked back down at the plotting board he had been neglecting on his lap. He was making plans, Kay thought, and she was awake enough to want to know what they were.

"Where are we?" she asked, wiping with the heel of her hand a crusty piece of sleep from her left eye. Will gave her some dried meat and fruit, and while she chewed slowly, he gathered up the plotting stones, stowing them in his cloak.

"It's not so much where we are as when we are," he answered. "We're going back in time."

Kay's eyes widened, and her arms shot out to hold on to the seat and the metal casing of the plane to either side of her. She suddenly felt the precariousness of a plane that was floating on the air hundreds of meters above the ground, and falling all the time.

"Only in a manner of speaking!" Will cried, laughing over the drone of the engines. "We're going back to a time when imaginers ruled the world, and this was their capital city!"

Just then, the little plane banked hard to the left, and Kay could see over Will's head the shimmering, sunlit vision of a white city, laid out on the coast just below them. Fronting the blue waters of a wide bay, it nearly toppled over with white buildings and green palms, heaped up along avenues that shot back from the sculpted seaside. To the right, a promenaded waterfront stretched for miles to a busy harbor, broken up by sandy bars and beaches where a few people walked.

Kay noticed some of them were pointing at the plane as it dropped.

Without meaning to, she held out her finger and pointed back. Will smiled.

"Isn't it glorious?" he shouted.

Now the plane began its descent in earnest, even as it arced in the opposite direction, for a long and breathless span seeming to dangle Kay over the blue water of the sea.

"You're going to have to keep your face covered," Will said to her, barking his words over the rush of air and engines, "or we may attract attention. You'll need to wear this." He pulled out from beneath the seat a loose cotton robe and passed it over to her. "See if you can put it on under the straps. We'll be on the ground very soon." Kay sat upright, and with some inventive contortions got the robe over her head, pulling the hood down the back of her neck and drawing up the ends of the fabric belt to lie ready in her lap. As the plane descended, she caught sight of a bright sea heaving broadly into the distance to their right. Immediately she swiveled round to the left and peered—as much as she could—over the lip of the seat.

A moment before, looking out the other way, she had been

able to see only water and sky. But from this direction the view was very different. A massive city loomed behind the ocean to her left—

"We'll have to stow this thing on the beach," Will called out merrily, just as Flip cut down in a last swoop to the broad, flat sand and rock that had been exposed by the tide. "By the air, through the air!" he whooped, waving his long arm in the sky. After a few awkward bounces that made Kay's heart shake, the plane was light enough to settle and run itself out, pulling up short and with a sudden exhalation of noise opposite a boarded-up beach house. Kay and Will clambered out and jumped down, and Flip stowed the little plane unobtrusively between a long, crumbling shore wall and a set of beach shacks. Kay got the sense that the two wraiths had done all this before. *Whatever* this *is.*

"Are we going into the city?" she asked Will. He was sweeping sand from his cloak.

He held her eyes in his the length of a look. Then he asked her, "Have you seen a mushroom before?"

She nodded.

"Describe it."

Using her fingers and fumbling for words, Kay began to

shape the white dome of a mushroom, overhanging its woody stalk—

"No," Will cut in. Firm but gentle. "That's not the real mushroom at all. The real mushroom is below the ground. It is large. It lives for years and years. It spreads through the soil, sometimes across miles and miles. What you see above the ground, in comparison to that—it's almost nothing. The real fungus is hidden, massive, like an old story lost in time but still throwing up consequences. Those pretty little caps are just its fruits, like tiny apples hanging from a giant tree."

Kay tried to imagine an apple tree spreading across miles through the ground, bearing little mushroom fruits, upside down, that pushed through the soil into the grass. Flip joined them. He was wiping oil off his hands onto a rag.

"The city you see is like that, the fruit of a much larger, older, more important city. That real city, the huge one, extends down into the ground, like a mushroom, but also back into time. It has been there for centuries, growing, throwing forth new buildings and boulevards, new parks and people, in an ongoing evolution of itself. *That* city, the real one, the ancient one, the stalk and trunk of which this"—he gestured before him—"is just the fruit: that's the city we're going to. The city of imaginers, which you can only reach by dreaming."

"The mushroom talk," said Flip, nodding with mock sagacity. "Very philosophical, Will."

Will elbowed Flip in the ribs.

"Ow!" cried Flip merrily.

"Fair," judged Kay. "And these imaginers—will be able to help us?"

The wraiths had been laughing. Now their faces settled, fast, like long grass flattening before a wind. "No one better," said Will. "Trust me." He offered her his hand. Kay took it.

They walked up the beach toward the city. Kay's short legs had to work double-time to keep up with Will and Flip, and in the bright sun the white buildings seemed for a long time to hang out of reach. Finally the two wraiths led her off the beach onto a cobbled alleyway that ran down between low houses into a larger square. From that point on, the city became more and more congested with buildings, pedestrians, noise, activity, cars and, above all, smells. Kay could taste alternately the acrid, then sweet, then again acrid waves of bus exhaust against the sweet of street vendors. Ripe garbage rotted in the heat on one corner, and at the next a woman drenched in perfume hailed a taxi. It must be morning, Kay decided, in this new and frenetic place, and, despite the worry that gnawed at her, she had to admit she loved it. All the noise and talk, the bustle and haste, the joyful energy of the street absorbed her into its rhythm, and she felt she was bouncing in time with it as they strode through the waking city. *This,* she thought, was what it was to be alive—and not the quiet, somber fear of the mountain, the subdued flows of murmuring wraiths, the still and empty halls.

But as they walked, she noticed that the wraiths did not seem to love it at all: they walked stiffly, their heads constantly swerving this way and that as they took in the crowds, the motion and, it might be, the threat around them. Kay felt no threat. She had never felt so glad to be free, to be walking, to be among people and noise and bustle. She caught a flash of herself in a shop window as they passed by and, without even quite meaning to, straightened her back and began to saunter. *Take that, whatever place you are.* She almost giggled—and crashed directly into a woman who had been hurrying past them, a daughter held tightly in each hand.

"Oh, I'm sorry," Kay said, blushing red and drawing back the hood of her robe.

Will turned, scowling, but the startled woman looked at

her uncomprehendingly and said something out of the corner of her mouth that Kay could not understand at all. And then, beneath her brown curls, one of the little girls began to cry. Kay stared at her, and she cried harder. She looked at the mother, then at the girl.

Ell. Mum. What am I doing?

The thoughts intruded so swiftly and suddenly they nearly robbed Kay of her breath. She felt in her stomach that giddy absence she had felt as the plane was diving, and her legs, suddenly turned to jelly, buckled beneath her.

Dad. The sight of his mucky, bloody, ravaged face swam before her eyes, and though she knew very little, she knew her body, out of control, was swaying on the pavement. She felt sick.

Will got behind her then, and steered her—gently but firmly. Now she was walking between the two gaunt forms, blocked in from the rush of sometimes inquisitive faces passing them on the pavements. But Kay had stopped noticing. Her thoughts raced, counting evenings and mornings since she and Ell had climbed from their bedroom window. *Nine days left. Nine days to find you.* And then, without warning, Will took her hand and, in the same motion, veered left under a low, dark archway, ducking gracefully and pulling Kay down a dim stone staircase. It was slick with dripping water, and she almost stumbled several times as they went down, down, down.

At the bottom, in almost complete darkness, she stopped before a worn, blackened slab of stone, in which a few mysterious words had been cut, their clear capitals still legible against the murk.

ALEXANDRIA WATER COMPANY

Kay turned toward the light of the stair, and Will's black shape against the light behind her.

"Alexandria," she said. "But that's in another country altogether. That's in —"

"Egypt," he answered. "We flew a long way during the night."

Everything in Kay's body, everything in her heart and on the tip of her tongue, all that she could feel or think dropped like lead shot into her feet; and she stood rooted to the ground as if she were a yew, or a cypress, or some enormous, dark and silent tree.

We're so far away. Ell. Only nine nights left.

Will sat lightly on a slick step, and now Kay could see his

face, gentle and pained. Flip had gone on ahead; she could hear him knocking or shaking what sounded like a metal door. The last of the exuberance she had felt up on the street now curdled in her stomach, and she grew dizzy, as if she were sliding slowly into a bottomless hole.

"There's only one way we can get your sister back, Kay, and your father. And the wraith who can help us is here. He left the mountain a long time ago—the last of the imaginers to hold out against Ghast. He hated Ghast. He still hates Ghast. And Ghast still fears him. This, Alexandria, is where he came to hide." Will paused and looked at his hands, palms down in front of him. "Ghast wants him dispersed. His wispers are always searching for Phantastes."

Beside him water trickled down the heavy, square stones of the wall and ran among the outcroppings of furzy moss and slime. Kay watched the little beads collecting, then running and dispersing, then collecting again as they raced down the rough dark stone. At the top of the wall the stones were damp, uniformly wet all over; at the bottom, little dropping rivulets fed a whispering current in a gulley running down. Kay looked again and again over the wall, trying to find the place where the dampness became a rivulet. It was right there, but she couldn't see it.

"Phantastes is—well—" Will stopped for a moment and looked down at Kay seriously. "When someone has an idea—I mean, a really *new* idea—it has to come into being somehow. You have to create a thing that wasn't there before. From nothing, something. The more you think about it, the more impossible it seems. Now, dispersal—what Ghast did to your father—is absolute. He's gone. It's as if he never was. It's the reverse of an idea. Where there was something, now there is nothing. Where there was someone, now there is no one at all."

Kay felt a wail stiffening in her chest. Will put his hand gently on her shoulder, and together they held her together.

"But what Phantastes can do—integration—is also absolute. If anyone can find your father, if anyone can help us bring him back to himself, Phantastes can. He's really the only hope we have. And that's exactly why Ghast is afraid of him."

"And what about Ell?" said Kay, clenching her fists at her sides.

"I don't know. But this is where we can find help, Kay. I know it."

"In the . . . sewer?"

Will smiled. "Phantastes is still alive because no one knows how to find him. Because he lives in the real Alexandria, the one that lies beneath and behind the one everyone else can see. Because the only way to reach him is to lose yourself in this maze of dark and ancient tunnels half drowned in water. But if you come down here and you get lost in just the right way, he usually finds you."

"Usually?" Kay asked.

Flip came running round the corner. "Five minutes," he said breathlessly. "We've got to be very, very fast."

Kay didn't even have a moment to look confused.

"Come on." Will grabbed her by the hand and loped after Flip, who had already disappeared back round the corner.

They ran as best they could along the low passages and through several doors that, Kay realized as they swept through each one, Flip had probably just opened. Each one seemed to have a heavy lock, and Flip impatiently clanged each one shut behind them before they set off again. The tunnels were hot, and water dripped everywhere around them, so that as they ran, Kay began to feel like she was racing through a greenhouse in the dark, or some dense and tropical swamp. In the occasional shafts of light from above she could see moss growing down ancient cobbled walls, and at intervals, stone arches just tall enough for her to pass through. And always, beneath her feet, a little water, several inches deep in places, only scattered trickles and puddles in others.

"Any time now, Will," Flip muttered under his breath as he raced ahead, ducking under an arch to the next door. He called over his shoulder, "Two more doors!"

They were through them in a few moments, and as they stood on the far side of the second, in the lowest and darkest of the tunnels yet, Kay could hear a rushing sound.

"It's the flush," Will said as they spun on their heels and set off again. "The city sewers flush with river water at periodic intervals during the day."

The tunnel ended abruptly in a huge, cavernous underground lake, and Kay, still thinking with forward velocity, nearly tumbled into it. Only with difficulty did she manage to stop and step back from the edge of the pavement. The lake before them looked dark, and it smelled faintly revolting.

"For centuries—since the Romans—Alexandria's cisterns have been fed by canals from the Rosetta Nile, but the canals also supply the major sewers. The waste is flushed into this lake," Will finished.

Flip was sitting in a small boat that Kay hadn't noticed at first, off to the side of the long landing. He held two oars that were poised in the locks, their blades hanging inches above the fetid water.

"In!" said Will.

Keeping their bodies low, they both scrambled into the boat; the oars dropped, and Flip, sitting opposite Kay, began to pull at them with the strength and regularity of a piston. Kay turned to Will, her eyes full of wordless questions about what was happening, and why, and where they were; but he was paying no attention. Instead he was looking back toward the landing; and when she followed his gaze, she saw why.

A meter of foaming green water suddenly began to pour through open grates around that last door, down the passage and into the lake behind them. Kay gasped to think how, if they had been only seconds slower, they might have been caught in its thundering force. It poured and poured, a cataract of color and motion. As the water flooded through the grilles, and from other doors along the wall of the cavern, a surge began to push into the lake, lifting the boat along as Flip rowed away into the gloom.

Will held his finger to his lips. "Not one word," he mouthed.

Kay looked around as they surged rhythmically across the

black, silty lake. Above them a dome of rock hung in shadow, here and there perforated by weak and dusky lights—slipped stones, or drains running from the streets above, Kay thought as she craned her head to look over her shoulder. Water dripped from the ceiling in places, and as they passed across the surface, the loud plinks fell around the boat in a random pattern.

Now the far shore began to loom out of the gray light. It was much like the one they had left. A long landing perched a couple of meters above the water. Kay couldn't quite pull herself up without help and, as there was no ladder, she was grateful for Will's quick lift. The two wraiths were up in an instant, jumping so lightly from the little skiff that it didn't even rock behind them.

While the wraiths moored the boat, Kay walked on ahead through a low, open archway that led off the landing. Beyond was an ancient passage, bathed in light from above. The gate to the passage stood unlocked and swung wide with a slight push, so Kay simply walked through it. No sooner had she stepped across the threshold, turning toward the mossy cobbles of the wall with her hand outstretched, than the heavy iron gate slammed shut behind her. She knew without turning that it was locked. She froze, then spun and grabbed the gate, trying to shake it free. Her stomach heaved into her throat.

Flip was there in three instant bounds. He spoke almost without breathing, in a torrent of exact, unforgettable words, the most urgent thing anyone had ever said to her. "You have between three and four minutes until the next flush. It *will* drown you if you are caught in it. The doors ahead of you are locked. There is no way you can get through them. Don't waste time trying. You are going to have to find another way. Wherever you end up, make noise. A lot of noise. We will find you. Go now."

Kay stood at the gate, gripping its iron bars as hard as she had gripped anything before in her life. She stared into Flip's eyes, and he into hers. Neither one of them would let go.

"Go!" He was shouting at her. "Go! Go, go!"

Kay turned and sprinted straight ahead. Before she had gone twenty paces, the abundant light began to fail and she was soon in near-total blackness. She held her hands out in front of her and tried to keep running straight; and for two or three paces she seemed to manage it, slowly, stumblingly. Then, feeling her way along the wall to the right, she advanced more slowly. The tunnel curved, and the stone was rough and wet under her hands. A grayness took shape in front of her, then around her, and she thought she saw light coming through cracks in the high ceiling above. She tried to remember the water she had seen earlier, which had run not much more than a meter deep. If she could just climb clear of it, she could wait it out or get up to those cracks, and—who could say?—maybe she could get out.

She put her hands on the wet walls and tried to dig her fingers into the cobbles. She managed to get moss under her nails but couldn't find any purchase. Again, and again, and again she tried, first with her hands, reaching, and then with her feet. Desperation made her foolish, and she scrabbled at the wall to no avail at all—it was too slick, the stones were too shallowly set, and she hadn't the strength. She began to cry and, as the tears ran, her chest threw up big jerking sobs. Now she couldn't see a thing, and her arms went suddenly limp. She dropped to the floor and let her head sink against the wall.

I am going to drown.

But her head wasn't leaning against the wall. It had hit something metal, something iron, something very painful.

Scrambling round, she found that it was a low grille set into the cobbles, covering a kind of duct or channel.

Of course. The water has to flow out of the passage. Drains.

She crouched and felt her way down the wall, finding more grilles, hoping for a loose one. There were more. She was counting them off, darting from grille to grille, when she realized that the gathering roar around her ears was the flush, already upon her, pouring from up ahead, from above.

Seconds. I have seconds.

Kay groped furiously, looking for any way out of the tunnel. Her pulse roared in her ears and she felt light—as light as a leaf. *Here, Kay*—she felt as if someone were speaking to her, leading her from stone to stone. The hair stood erect on the back of her neck as an electric charge surged from her core to her fingertips. *Faster,* said the voice. *Faster.*

Then her hand hit nothing in the darkness—a gap in the wall, large and open. She remembered the water she had seen earlier, pouring from the wall—surely—through just such a hole. Without further thought she dropped to her knees, kicked out her feet and tipped herself into it. She slid down a steep slope as if it were coated in butter.

It seemed a long while that she endured the sometimes

precipitous slide, her elbows jarring and knocking against the rough edges of the duct. She didn't dare to open her eyes or take her hands away from her face. The rushing sound had died away, but she knew that the water might engulf her at any time. *Calm before the storm.* She flailed desperately every time her feet got caught up on some obstacle or lip in the stone. Her back felt as if it were being pounded with blunt wooden hammers, and her neck ached as she strove to lift her head just far enough off the duct floor to avoid knocking.

Then, very suddenly, she came to a complete stop. She was level, flat, stuck. With her hand pressed against stone only inches from her face, she knew she was still enclosed in the narrow duct; and now she could hear the water again—higher pitched this time, but rising in volume. She thrust her hands out sideways and grappled for a hold, then pushed herself forward; the floor of the duct was just slick enough to let her continue to slide. On and on, her joints nearly tearing with the strain, she pushed, gasping for breath, until she felt her feet come clear of the ground, no longer beneath her—and then her legs, and then, very nearly, her back.

She could see nothing at all, though her eyes gaped open in the rising breeze rushing down the tunnel. The water was almost upon her. She flipped over onto her stomach, pushed herself out, and hoped that there would be a floor somewhere below.

She dropped.

In that last moment before she let go, Kay had imagined a ledge, another plinth or landing like the one she had seen a few minutes before on the lake shore above. What she hit, only a meter below her dangling legs, surprised her. It felt like earth: a little rocky, but there was a squelch of mud under her shoes, too. Any second now the flush would pour out of the duct. *One. Two. Three.* Then she heard it gushing; she listened hard. It sounded as if water were pouring not just out of here, but all around a very vast space. Unlike in the cavern above, here the vault seemed to echo emptily with the draining and dripping of what sounded like a hundred spouts. Slowly, her hands still pressed to the wall, she turned round to face outward, keeping her feet close, just in case.

To her relief, a gray gloom lit the space in front of her so that she was able to make out the main contours of another great cavern—exactly like the one from which she had just fallen except, judging by the apparent height of the vault, much larger. Behind her, as she clambered away, the drain began to pour with water, and she could hear, if not see, the water streaming down the slope to another great lake. The lake was so wide and the cavern so gloomy that she couldn't see across to the other side; her vision hit the obscurity like a wall. Kay stared for a long time, happy to be on her feet, relieved to have escaped drowning in the flush, but anxious about what this cavern contained, and how she was to get out of it. Flip had said that he and Will would find her. *He told me to make noise.* She took a deep breath. *Well then, I will make noise.*

She sang. At first she tried songs she had learned at school—quietly, almost under her breath, hardly daring to project herself into the darkness, only occasionally, on the refrains, letting a few bold notes out into the resounding dark. After a few minutes she had begun to find her voice, and the melodies started to soar a little, out into the higher pitches of the cavern's domed ceiling. Having run through all the songs from the school choir, Kay paused and breathed while she tried to remember the longer and more beautiful songs that her father had taught her. She sang the first phrase that came into her head and, closing her eyes as she had so often done while he lullabied his two daughters to sleep, she let his words well up and pour out:

The blue light rose like a flower in the night
when my true love came to me;
she laid her left hand in my right,
and the nightingale sang in the silkworm tree,
to me, when she came to me.

Had never holy mountain height
nor so dread deep the sea
as the love my true love did me plight
when the nightingale sang in the silkworm tree,
to me, when she came to me.

Then let the loose leaves laugh with delight
and tremble my love to see
where she rises like morning new, and bright,
and let the nightingale sing in the silkworm tree,
to me, for she comes to me.

With her chin lifted and eyelids softly set, Kay had drifted into that state perched just over sleep in which, so many nights before, she had listened to her father sing those words and heard them in her own head. She didn't know, nor did she worry now, whether she understood the words, or even what they were, so drowsy and warm had she become. As she sang, it was as though she was following her voice into all the reaches of the vault, where it flew and bounced and then, rebounding on the water and the walls, bounced again. Well before she came to the last verse she felt that she, like her song, had grown as large as the cavern—or maybe that the cavern itself was singing, and she was only standing in it, a note like any other in its huge, enduring, dark music.

When she reached the end of the song, for a long moment she stood quietly; and in that silence she was suddenly aware of another sound, a sound that was not the song, and she opened her eyes. It was the whispering swish of a pole in the water, not twenty meters from where she stood on the shore. As she followed it up with her eyes from the surface of the lake, in the gloom, the muscles tightened up her spine, gathering into a compact, rising knot like the fist of a flower: there before her on the lake was a flat boat, and in the boat stood a tall, gaunt old wraith. In his right hand the pole, in his left a large brown book. He was bearded, part brown and part white, and his hair tumbled wispily, too, down over his shoulders. Like the other wraiths, he wore a hooded gray-black gown, the hood slung low around his shoulders and back, and the front loosely open over his white shirt. He was barefoot, Kay noticed. For a time he did nothing at all; he simply watched her, without staring, as if she were a tree and he were lying in the grass beneath her, looking up through her trembling leaves.

And then, abruptly, he spoke, in a voice so clear and yet so soft that Kay was surprised she could hear him, let alone understand him.

"So you are here at last." He paused for a long time, still picking out the blue of a spring sky between her breeze-tossed branches. "Before I was born, that song had already been sung in my family for a thousand years or more. We handed it down from generation to generation, each one teaching the next. My mother sang it to me when I nursed at her breast, and I had it with her milk. When I was a boy, running barefoot through the fertile fields of Assyria, I thought that if I could just run as fast as the wind, I might see the Bride; if I could just burn as hot as fire, she would come to me; if I could just beat upon the rooftops as hard as the autumn rain, she would lull me to sleep in her arms. I wished more than anything to be a storyteller, to become a singer of tales. Well. It took me thirty years to sing that song: an age of man. An age of man to become a man; an age of man to learn that I must sit still to be moved, must close my eyes to see, must give myself up to discover who I am. And yet now, in this time of children who have lost the oldest art, who cannot sit, who cannot close their eyes, who cannot for even a moment surrender their too-cherished selves, in such an age, a child now sings this song to me." He watched her again.

Kay stood stock-still, hands folded loosely across her chest.

"Tell me your name," he said softly.

"Katharine," said Kay. "My name is Katharine Worth-More."

The old man smiled broadly, revealing a thousand furrows in his lean cheeks, above his eyes, and between his mouth and chin. "Yes. Katharine," he answered. He shifted his weight onto the pole, and drove the boat slowly in to the shore where she stood. "And I am Phantastes, the last imaginer," he said as the front of the long punt began to grate against the rocky soil of the ground before Kay's feet. "Or very nearly the last."

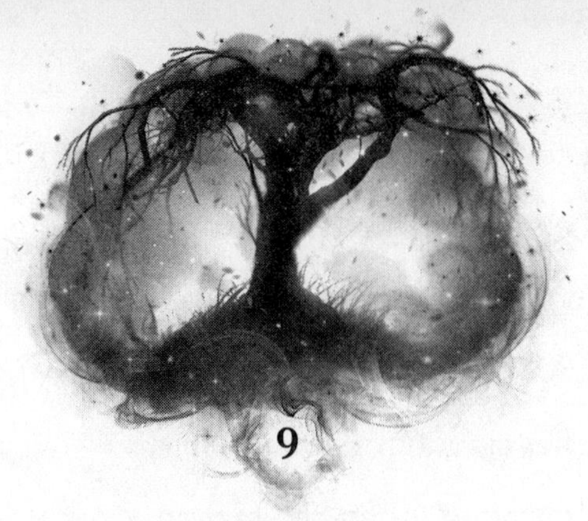

9

A Miracle

Guiding the boat across the underground lake, Phantastes pulled up alongside a cleft in the rock where water cascaded continuously from a gap very high up. It was a clean, clear stream, diverted, said the old wraith, from a reservoir. Kay doused her hair and washed her hands and face, and then Phantastes pushed the boat back out into the lake and made for the far shore.

Alert now, and shivering, Kay saw a small island—not big enough for five people to stand on, she thought. In its center stood the massive remains of a giant tree, jagged and broken, thrusting up toward the ceiling.

"What is it?" she asked. "Trees don't grow under the ground. How did this get here?"

Phantastes continued gently guiding the boat toward the island. "When this tree first germinated, no more than a seedling, it stood in the middle of a low lagoon, a place where the Nile canals flooded with fresh water a wide area of low-lying marshland. It was only thousands of years later that the silt, constantly collecting around this place, enclosed it and then buried it. Long before that, the great vaulted roof that"—and here he turned his head upward, leaning on the long pole and gesturing with his arm to take in the whole cavern—"you do not see above you was built: one of the grandest, most beautiful temples ever designed, and the crowning architectural achievement of a great society. Of course, no one else now knows that it is here, or that it is of such antiquity. Only I know."

Kay cocked her head to the left. "But they *must* know. I came down that duct from the sewage tunnel—someone must have built that."

The boat made no sound at all as it drew up on the shore of the island. Phantastes held out his hand to help Kay ashore. Their quiet movements felt like reverence.

"Did you think that was a sewer?" the old wraith answered, smiling as he took a seat on one of the gnarled roots of the old trunk. "No, it was no duct that brought you here. No common sewer. The water that flows into the temple lagoon through that passage is a little purer than that. I dug it out myself, and lined it with grouted stone. It took me many years." He paused and looked at his withered hands where they rested gently, one upon the other, on his lap. "But I'm pleased you thought it was a drain. No one had ever noticed it until you slipped down it."

Kay looked closely at his face, which was level with her own as she stood a meter or so away, at the edge of the tiny island. The skin beneath his eyes had become cockled over the years, gathering up into the inner corners by his hooked nose and radiating out in loose folds across cheeks that ridged up when he smiled. Even when he frowned he seemed kind, as if the frown were a comma between two smiles. "But all that time you must have spent digging it out," she said at last, voicing the question on which she had paused to regard him. "Why did you do it?"

"Because when I arrived here all this was dry. For thousands of years before that, this marshland had been kept wet—even under the dome of the great temple—by the flooding of the Nile; but at last the silt, covering over the hidden temple, had cut the water off completely. And when the city above began to leach so much of the water away, and then other cities upstream; and fields, with their irrigation projects, and who knows what else—houses, swimming pools—then the marsh died completely. And if it hadn't been for me"—and he patted the root on which he sat—"all this would have died, too."

"But surely it *is* dead," said Kay. "It's an old stump."

At this Phantastes looked up sharply, his mouth suddenly set hard. Then he softened, and his eyes flattened as he smiled again, and he said, rising, "Come look."

Just opposite where he had been sitting, out of sight of the boat, a deep gash in the old trunk ran almost to the ground, making a jagged, steep *V*. The brittle husk and shell of the old tree was more than five centimeters deep, and within that Kay thought there was nothing.

"Look inside," said Phantastes quietly, and he stood back so that she might climb up onto one of the roots and negotiate a passage for her head between the two steeply sloping edges of the trunk. At first it was so dark that she thought she was looking down a well, or into the earth itself; but after a few moments her eyes adjusted to the near darkness and she could just make out, faintly, five hand-sized, oval leaves that were perhaps green, reaching out from a central stem that was thirty centimeters or more in height. It shot out from a crack in the weathered wood of the center of the trunk, about a meter in diameter, and grew straight upward. Kay hastily pulled her head out of the hole, bumping herself painfully on the right ear as she spun round too soon.

"But how is it growing *here*? It's so dark!"

"It is the deepest well that holds the freshest water. Wait a few moments," Phantastes said, "and you will see the other little alteration I made to the Great Temple of Osiris."

Kay stood there, leaning against the side of the cleft trunk, her heart beating fast. The great sun god of the ancient Egyptians. Osiris. For years she had heard the stories at bedtime, all of them: Osiris's enmity with his brother, Set; his murder and dismemberment; the long and patient search of his wife, the goddess Isis, with the erection of a thousand temples all over Egypt. Her discovery of her husband's body in a cedar box lying at the center of a magnificent tree.

But that tree was in—

Kay looked up in confusion.

"Byblos," said Phantastes. Curiosity and surprise flashed like a pulse of light across his face. Kay had felt it, too: a brief unison or harmony, as if for a moment their thoughts had—impossibly—become the same. But it was only an instant, and then the feeling passed.

"Yes," he continued, "I know it was in Byblos. But the priests of Osiris took a cutting from that tree and planted it here, at the very center of the temple, in the marsh where the goddess later buried his body. And its roots grew down into his flesh, and it towered within the temple, the tips of its branches scraping against the stones of the vault above."

"But how?" Kay said as a sense of the sanctity of this place began to dawn upon her. "How did the tree grow inside the temple? Didn't it need light? Doesn't *this* tree need light?" She paused, staring at Phantastes. He said nothing. "A tree can't grow in a cave, underground."

"Look," he said at last, tilting his chin upward to the vault.

She followed his eyes with her own. For some reason she could not explain, her heart was hammering in her chest. The air was lightening very slightly around the cavern, and for the first time she could see the whole vault above. But she was totally unprepared for what happened next. A narrow beam of light suddenly flared from a hole in the roof, straight down the center of the shaft of the gigantic old stump, and illuminated the tiny plant growing at its center. Kay watched in wonder as the beam of light seemed to grow in intensity, transforming the little patch of wood at the center of the stump from which the sapling sprang into a tiny, brilliant piece of daylight. It went on for about five minutes, during which she tried to stop time, to draw it out, to take in more of the deep, woody greenness of the tiny plant, the delicate hairs bristling under its five fanning leaves, the glistening luminescence of its taut stem.

This is the most beautiful thing I have ever seen. It's miraculous.

But then, as abruptly as it had begun, it ended, and the darkness again put out the light. Tears started in Kay's dimmed eyes. The sight of that struggling, tiny stem with its delicate, childlike leaves—bathed in light—cast back into the darkness—it was too much.

"Five minutes a day is all I could manage," said Phantastes quietly as he put his hand on her head. "Mirrors, mathematics, trial and error—and I still can't do more than five minutes. But do not cry. It's enough."

Kay turned and sat heavily on the upper roots. It hadn't felt like five minutes.

"It took me many years even to get that much. And that was before I knew for sure whether the tree still had life in it.

Although I always suspected that it did," he said, patting the desiccated trunk with his mottled, gray-veined hand. "First I had to find a little money—here and there—and then drive some people from their homes, which I did not much enjoy. It was necessary to demolish many buildings while I looked for the right place to dig. And then, after I finally found it, I lost many more years in making mirrors and glasses to focus the light. It doesn't work perfectly even now, and it doesn't last long, but the leaves get a little bit of light every morning. And with the river washing into the temple several times a day now, the conditions are improving. Who knows but, a few years from now, this green stem may grow thick and stout enough to bear its own fruit—the shellfruit of the tree of Byblos, whorled like the shuttle, each one a rife and mysterious trove of tiny seeds, and in every seed the promise of new life, new growth, stems, trunks, a thousand branches, leaves and fruit, harvest on harvest past imagining. All that may be. But for now, it is just enough."

Kay was crying quietly.

"Child," said the old wraith. "Even small, delicate things can sometimes be remarkably resilient."

For no reason she could name, all Kay's urgency suddenly

came striking back into her heart and lungs, pressing down on her chest like heavy stones. The sorrow that had been in her eyes suddenly gripped her heart, and she thought of Ell, remembered her father, remembered her mother at home, sitting at her desk behind the closed door of her room, sobbing quietly the night before they left—the night before Christmas. Where was she now? What had she thought when she woke up the next morning to find her daughters gone? What had she made of Kay's hastily scrawled note? *We are going to find Dad. We will be back soon. We love you,* she had written, crammed in tiny letters on the back of Will's card and left in the middle of Ell's neatly made bed. Suddenly Kay felt she couldn't breathe at all. She choked; although the choke sounded more like a sob. "Why am I here?"

She spoke before she meant to. Her voice echoed for a few moments, and then there was silence.

Phantastes sat down next to her on the stump.

"Kay," he said, and his tone was much more familiar now, no more the tall and commanding presence he had been. He held out the palm of his right hand, extended before her. It seemed wonderfully still, open and capacious. Her eye was drawn instantly to its center where the lines crossed, where the contour of finger, sinew, muscle and callus produced a slight cupping or hollow. "I am not one of those wraiths who plots people's movements, as if a man or a woman or a child were no more than a little knot of likelihoods. I am an imaginer. For better or for worse, I understand the insides of things. Tell me what is in your heart."

Kay wanted to tell him what they had lost. She wanted to tell him about sitting at the kitchen table at home, where the lamp swung from the ceiling and gave a warm, golden glow. She wanted to tell him how her parents were seated opposite her, her mother gently stroking the back of her father's hand while he read a book and she, with a pencil in the other hand, planned a new painting—a big one—sketching out ideas and themes on page after page of her notebook. She wanted to tell him how Ell liked to pretend that she had homework, too, so that at the end of the evening, when Kay presented her books to her parents, she and her sister could disappear upstairs together to play.

But it was all so *normal*. Everything they had lost was so *normal*.

One by one these things had slipped away: first her parents had begun to quarrel, and no one stroked the back of anyone's hand. The notebook her mother had lost, or put in a drawer.

Then her father—he was always out working late, or away on some trip, and Kay was forever in her room, making lists of things she planned to do, or things she didn't have and wanted. And Ell stood in the kitchen, turning the light on and off, over and over, until no one could stand her. *Why did she do that?*

Kay wanted to tell Phantastes all this.

"I've lost my home," she said.

Phantastes was silent a moment. Then she saw that he had put his hand to his heart.

"I think I know how that feels," he said.

"Do you?"

"I have lost all my homes," answered Phantastes. "First I lost my home here, then Bithynia, too, was taken. And lastly I was driven from the mountain. Maybe that is a little like what you have lost."

"I lost my father, then my mother—how we were, I mean, the way we were *together.* And now they've taken my sister. No, that's not right. I let her go. I lost her. It was because I wasn't watching. I thought it was all about *me.* I let her go. I let all of them go."

Phantastes's reply was swift. "No, Katharine. It's not your fault."

"But I'm still the only one who can get them back. I'm the only one who can make it right. And I don't know how. I feel like I'll never get to go home again. Not to the home I want. Not to the home where we were together."

"Your father said much the same thing to me once, in this very place."

Kay looked up sharply, her chin cutting a slicing angle against her neck. "He did? How do you—"

"Do you think I do not know your father?" Kay stared at him in mute unimagining. "Do you think he and I have not walked in the moonlight on the sands of Alexandria? That he and I have not sailed against the wind off the coast of Anatolia? That he and I have not gathered mulberries in Grecian groves? No, child, your father and I are old friends, colleagues and sworn brothers in a struggle far greater than you have yet glimpsed or imagined. A struggle in which Ghast is, has always been, our greatest and most dangerous enemy. And why do you think Ghast wanted your father dispersed, if not because he knew that Ned More was working for me?"

"Working for you?" Kay asked, her mouth hanging open. Her lips, like her eyes, felt numb.

"Among the right-wraiths, your father is known as the

Builder. For years he has been excavating around the site of the ancient—and neglected—seat of the Honorable Society of Wraiths and Phantasms in Bithynia—"

Kay nodded with vigor. This was something she recognized. The Fragments Project. "He's an archeologist," she said.

"Yes, an archeologist . . ." Phantastes sounded dubious, and blew through his lips. "But he isn't working on it as an archeologist. No, your father is not studying the place because he wants to understand the past; he is rebuilding it because he wants to shape its future."

"But Will said that Bithynia was lost. Forever."

"Will does not yet know. It would be too dangerous to tell him because, above all others, Ghast keeps him under constant watch."

"Watch?" asked Kay. "Why?"

Phantastes stirred the water at the edge of the little island with the pole, which he had taken up again from where it was leaning against the old trunk. "Will may fumble sometimes. He may seem a little meek, a little broken. But do not underestimate him. There is no finer wraith in the mountain."

Then why doesn't he help me?

"We must help him."

Kay's whole body stiffened. Even in the low light, Phantastes saw it.

"We will find your sister, Katharine. And your father. We will save him. We will do it together. But to bring the Honorable Society back to Bithynia, to save Will from Ghast—this is what Ned More wants, too. You must help me now to keep Will safe, for he above all is in great danger. And you must help me to keep something else safe. It is far too dangerous for me to hold on to it." Here Phantastes leaned down to the boat and retrieved the book he had been holding before, when Kay first glimpsed him coming out of the darkness of the cavern. Only it could not be a book because, after unhooking a tiny clasp, Phantastes had opened it to reveal a fist-sized, lustrous white object inside. The book was a box, she realized, and it held something very beautiful. In a couple of steps Phantastes was at her side, and he offered it to her.

"Take it," he said. "I left the mountain many years ago, fleeing from Ghast and his hatred. But I also left in order to protect this. It belongs to Will, but he wouldn't mind." He smiled, holding out the box again.

Kay took the softly shining, smooth object from inside the box, but cautiously, afraid it might be brittle like glass and break in her hands; or that it might be slippery, and drop to shatter on the small rocks at her feet. It was heavy enough, though, and she could grip it easily. She turned it over in her hands. It was whorled like a shell and bone-smooth, cool to the touch. Here and there it was studded with something that, in the light, might have proved to be a gem or diamond. As she turned it over, she noticed that it was perforated with tiny holes.

"Hold it up to your mouth," Phantastes said, "and blow."

She did as she was told. At first she did not find just the right aperture, but in a moment she could feel the wind forcing a passage into one of the many tiny gaps. A deep, sonorous drone came vibrating out of the stone, and rang in the cavern. The bones in her shoulders shook with the heavy, sugary resonance of the tone; it seemed, as her lungs began to exhaust themselves, that the vibrations were spreading down into her ribs, so that her whole torso began to quiver, and she fought for the note not to end. When at last it did, she suddenly held the glassy stone away from her mouth, scrutinizing it again, then tried a different hole. This time the pitch was higher, and it oscillated like a wave breaking on the shore. Another clashed like swords, high and metallic. Another moaned—the voice of a grieving father at the grave of his only child. She held the shell in astonishment.

"The voice of the shuttle," said Phantastes quietly. "And the first note you sounded was that of love."

"You want me to keep *this*?" she asked. It was the most beautifully made thing she had ever handled.

"Yes," he went on. "Yes, it should be you." He shook his bowed head slowly, and Kay saw a tear drop from the tip of his nose. But he looked up, his eyes shining, and held out the box for her to replace the shuttle. "Come," he said more briskly, stowing the box in the punt and taking up the pole again. Kay followed him, fluid with questions, and began asking them the moment she was seated, looking up at the old wraith as he pushed them round the island and toward the near shore behind it.

"Is the shuttle Will's, then?"

"I suppose neither he nor that worthless Philip has told you just who Will is," said Phantastes, grinning so that the etched lines of his face stretched, soaking in the inky light.

"No," Kay answered.

"Then we will let him tell you himself, in his own way. Next question."

"How did you know that Ghast had taken my sister and my father?"

"Not all the wispers are loyal to Ghast—even those he trusts most answer in their quiet ways to me. Despite themselves. I have been taking regular reports on him, and on you, for quite some time."

Phantastes grinned at her again, now so widely and impishly that his ears flexed. "Have a look at the top of the box there"—he gestured down below his feet to where the shuttle lay in its wooden case—"and I think you might put a few things together."

Kay looked. Carved into the dark wood of the lid was a shape which she had to trace with her finger before she could resolve it completely: a slender snake entwined with a sword. She knew that symbol. She looked up quickly. "Rex, the old porter at my father's office!"

"Is that how he hid himself?" Phantastes asked, chuckling. "Yes, he's one of mine. That was a clever ploy of his, yes. I sent him to recover several vital items, including that shuttle, from your father's study. Next question."

"Where has Ghast taken my father and my sister? How do we get them back?"

Phantastes didn't answer. They were almost at the shore and, with a wide sweep of the punt pole, he gracefully swung the boat parallel with the long stone plinth onto which they both stepped. Kay turned to him as he secured the boat and retrieved the shuttle, and to his hunched back said, "I mean it. Where are they?"

Phantastes rose quickly and set off along the wall at a brisk pace, Kay tripping at his side. "I cannot imagine," he said. "It is not so easy; Ghast and his acolytes could have taken your father anywhere. And yet, if they performed a full dispersal, he will not have ended up just anywhere. His dispersal will have been consummated in a place special to *him*, a place that springs from the individual nature of his own mind and experience." Phantastes turned on his heel and, squatting, placed his palm on the stone floor before Kay. "What do you know of integration?"

Kay's eyes widened. She shook her head. Words were whizzing so quickly by her, she wasn't sure she understood half of them.

"Everyone—everyone—is like a buried treasure. Everyone. Every person who has ever been born is inestimably valuable. You are. You are like a huge hoard of gold, jewels, spices—the richest stuff there is. But with this limitation: your treasure is buried, hidden, locked away somewhere and perhaps even you don't know where. The performance of a dispersal is a little like making a map: when a wraith performs a dispersal, she or he maps the whole life, the whole mind, the whole being of the subject—finds the treasure—and then goes to that place, to that thought, to that feeling, and digs it up. Destroys the treasure. An integration is the *reverse.* When we undo a dispersal, when we integrate, then we find a new place, and we make a treasure as great or greater than that which was destroyed, and we bury it again. Do you see?"

Phantastes's face was inches from her own. Kay thought of that gold and silver, those costly jewels and spices, pouring into the earth. She nodded.

"But I don't have long," Kay blurted out. "For making maps and digging and burying. I have nine nights left."

"Yes," Phantastes nodded. His mouth tightened. It almost clanged. "Ghast's little device. I heard that he has taken the Great Wheel, and mocks us. It is no matter. First we will have to find Will and Philip. I have a feeling they will be waiting for us in the compound above. I need to know one or two things before we can start making preparations for integration." He looked straight into Kay's eyes. "But we will find your father, and we will recover him."

Kay smiled. If Will always made her feel safe, Phantastes gave her hope.

The old wraith rose and set off at pace toward a low door; here a passage led off the landing. Kay followed, almost skipping. Her clothes had nearly dried in the warm drafts that stirred the cavern, and as she moved she felt suddenly light. They went up several slightly sloping tunnels, and through one or two open gates.

"The flush—" Kay began.

"Is finished for the day," Phantastes called over his shoulder. "Anyway, these passages do not connect to the sewerage system. These are the old corridors of the temple buildings, which I excavated and restored. And in a moment you can see my most ambitious work."

They went round a few tight corners, and then, without warning, passed through a low door into a huge, open atrium; round the outside a staircase spiraled upward as far as the eye could see.

"I confess I cheated a bit. We're actually inside an old tower—like everything else, engulfed by the silt—which I dug, or rather flushed, out. Well, dug *and* flushed. All the sediment that used to fill it is back in the lake," he said, "where it belongs. The stairs"—which they were already climbing—"were mostly already here. I made some improvements and repairs. It's a wonderful commute," he added, laughing over his shoulder at her: she was struggling to keep pace as they rose through the increasingly bright air toward the top. The atrium seemed to be narrowing as they climbed, until finally it was little more than a circular stone stairwell. Light came from the center of the roof—very close now—and Kay realized that it was the sun shining through a skylight, and that they had reached ground level again. Just under the skylight, a door stood shut; pulling a ring of keys from the belt beneath his robe, Phantastes quickly opened it. The heavy wood swung wide to reveal an ordinary white-walled room, with sunlight pouring in from two open windows on the left. It dazzled Kay's eyes, and she squinted to see the wooden trestle table standing in the center, and on it a pile of what looked like dried leaves. Around the walls, tall bookshelves sagged under masses of volumes of every size. This library, the table, the leaves, the great window looking onto the terrace—none of this detained her gaze.

Her eyes were elsewhere. The little domed ceiling, like

the walls everywhere between the tall cases, was covered with painted snakes of every size, writhing, slithering, muscular and scaled, composed in such brilliant, iridescent colors that Kay recoiled from the room, stumbling and throwing out her hand in stunned paralysis to catch at the door frame. Of all the contorted and entangled shapes that filled her vision, one above all had fixed itself in the center of her gaze, and—as she stared, helpless—it seemed to grow and grow, its fangs dripping with venom and its eyes with malice.

"Welcome to the last Imaginary," said Phantastes, spinning on his heel so that his long robe unfurled around him like the skirts of a dervish. "Welcome to my home. The place of poison. The place of healing. Do not draw back, child, but enter."

10

Integration

No sooner had Kay crossed into the little room than Phantastes closed the door behind her, and locked it. He replaced the keys at his belt just as a small, balding, wizened wraith scurried in through the door opposite and began to push the dried leaves into a heap, with the same motion setting down two or three heavy books and opening them. Phantastes slipped the shuttle into a little leather bag, and surreptitiously handed it to Kay behind the other wraith's back; then he joined him at the table, peering down at the huge folio volumes as the little man opened them and began, using a small rule, to scan through lines of heavily inked Gothic print. Kay dawdled awkwardly in the room's only shadow, eager to participate, and yet reluctant to put herself among the room's thousands of glistening, fanged mouths. She slung the leather bag over her shoulder, feeling the weight of its contents with pride and a little terror.

"Have you found it yet?" asked Phantastes. His voice was quiet, but not without authority and urgency.

Kay looked intently at the dark, almost hairless head as it pored over the books. The little wraith said nothing for a moment, but kept running his nimble hands back and forth across the lines of text, mumbling softly to himself. When he looked up at last, he blinked several times in the way someone might clear his throat. And then he cleared his throat.

"Nothing yet. But the maker is still at the fountain, and it may be that I have not remembered all that there is to recall."

"Keep listening to him," Phantastes said, setting his hand on the other wraith's slender arm. "It will come to him in time." The old wraith then turned round, indicating Kay with his arm, and said, "The young man's daughter. The Builder." The shrunken little wraith bowed with great ceremony. To Kay, Phantastes said, "Kay, this is our chronicler, Eumnestes. He will remember anything these forty thousand years. And remembering is the first part of integration."

And then, his duty done, the little wraith bustled out of the room again, the books tucked one under each arm.

"If remembering is the first part of integration," asked Kay, "what is the second?"

I remember my father well enough. But he is still gone.

"Sit down," said Phantastes gently, pulling out one of the four high-backed wooden chairs that stood around the table. "Perhaps I was wrong to speak to you about burying treasure. One should never pretend that difficult things are easy. It never helps."

"I'm not scared of difficult things," said Kay, taking the offered chair.

"Oh?" Phantastes was looking out the window of the little room, onto a kind of terrace. Outside, the sun was bearing down with searing intensity, but the broad leaves of vines and palms created shimmering shades around the stone window, and the air trembled with indecision, caught between heat and cool.

Kay was thinking of high, vaulted cathedrals, their ceilings fretted and roundeled by master masons hundreds of years dead; of complex music floating indistinctly on the air; of the fleeting intensity of incense that burned her eyes and made her throat dry. She didn't understand any of it—how it was made, what it meant or even how it made her feel—but she knew she loved it.

"It's said that the great conqueror Alexander, when he had subdued the known world, dismounted from his horse, laid his head upon the ground and wept—because there were no more worlds to conquer." Phantastes sighed. "Difficulty can be a blessing. Think how we should weep, like Alexander, if the world were to surrender all its mysteries."

Kay smiled. *There it was again. Hope.*

"The first part of integration is remembering," said Phantastes. "The second part is forgetting."

Kay might have spoken. She drew in a sharp breath.

"Any act of remembering is also an oblivion. Think. First, to remember one thing, one person, one thing about that person, we must forget a world of other things, a whole host of other people. To fix the mind in one place is to withdraw from every other. But there is a deeper mystery, too. When we remember a thing, or a person, we replace them—the real thing, the real person—with the memory. We *dis*place them. You would never say you remembered someone if he were standing before you."

Phantastes stood before her. Kay nodded.

"Dispersal destroys a human life. Integration restores it, but at a cost."

Phantastes spun round, his finger immediately dancing along the high shelves on the wall opposite. He was looking for something. When he found it and hefted it free, Kay saw that it was a large leather-bound book with gold letters tooled across the spine and cover. She had no time to look at the cover, though, because Phantastes had already cracked it wide open, and had begun to riffle through the ancient yellowed pages, mumbling as he went. Kay glimpsed handwritten English text framing beautiful illustrations in red, purple, blue and gold. Page after heavy page he turned, as Phantastes hunted through the volume. Finally he was satisfied and his hands stopped. "Ah," he said. "Listen."

"Tantalus was a very pious man, and when he came to be king, his piety, which had always been acknowledged by all, was heralded the known world over. He had an only son, a beautiful boy called Pelops. Poised between childhood and age, Pelops was full of promise, and that promise was of greatness. Tantalus heard the rumors of his son's goodness, his generosity, his courage, his quick intelligence, and he witnessed them with his own eyes, observing Pelops in his military exercise down by the stables, and

in the less sweaty but no less challenging labors set him by his tutors in arithmetic, composition, music and astronomy. Tantalus was excessively proud of his son, the more so because he had lost his wife in a hunting accident, leaving him without the possibility of further children. All his hope and his throne's future was tied up, by her death, in this boy; and he often thought it a marvel—as he watched him in conference with some of his councilors, or running in high spirits with a pack of hounds out of the castle grounds—that his own heart did not burst with pride."

Phantastes had become engrossed in his story, and with the heavy book still spread wide in his arms, he turned toward the window, and its warm light.

"It was with the most painfully anguished regret, then, that Tantalus received, and obeyed, the oracle sent him in his son's fourteenth year: that for the good of the nation, and for his own fame and honor, he should make his son a sacrifice to the gods of Olympus. Tantalus sent to the oracle once every year, and had many times in the past received replies that troubled or confused him; but always his piety led him through, and he considered the pain of his many penances and privations the proper price of good kingship. This time, however, he chewed bitterly over his instruction. Kill his own son! Could his piety rise even to this?

In the end, after a sleepless night, he resolved that the gods were indeed testing him, and that the sacrifice demanded was so total, so impossible, precisely because the Olympians were prepared to reward his fidelity with equal favor. When on the next day his son's blood was poured into the sacred vessels in the temple of Zeus Thunderer, he drew the knife himself.

"It may well have been a test; what man can know the mind of the gods? For certain we can say only that the outcome was not what he expected: within the year a famine raged in the country, a plague felled one out of every three householders, a terrible whirlwind and a tempest destroyed many of the great public buildings, including the temple of Zeus Thunderer—and Tantalus himself, his faith in the gods not only shaken but entirely consumed, withered and died of grief. His councilors, seeing the greater part of the Greek world thrown into disorder and suffering, sent again to the oracle, and received this answer: that there was a young man in Epidaurus, a son of Apollo, who could heal Pelops and return his body to life; and that, unless they brought him to do this, the whole of Lydia, of Greece and of Crete would be plunged into turmoil for a hundred years, and their own names wiped from the records of humanity.

"This Asclepius—for so he was called—was sent for, and

within a few days arrived, disembarking from Tantalus's ship at the head of a convoy of a hundred mules. Every one of these mules was laden with two baskets, and every basket contained a score of snakes, gathered from every variety across the known world. Many of the most potent venoms in the world are also, under different circumstances, powerful as medicinals and elixirs, and Asclepius beyond all others excelled in this snake lore. Alighting with his snakes at the ruined temple of Zeus, this son of Apollo called for the hewn limbs of Pelops to be brought to him as quickly as possible; thereafter he disappeared from public view, retreating into the deep impenetrability of the sanctum. All the people could see was that the snakes had been loosed, and they moved freely around the temple in their masses, transforming the place into a horror and convincing many of the citizens that they would escape the compound and infest the city. But they did not; and on the third day Pelops was seen to walk on his own feet out of the temple, through the agora, to his home in the castle. He ruled Lydia, Phrygia, Paphlagonia and most of Greece for sixty years; and Asclepius, traveling with freedom and royal warrant throughout his domains, created a name for himself as the greatest healer the world has ever known. It was in his schools that the great doctor Hippocrates first trained; and it was said that even Apollo, from whom all his arts of healing had been derived, eventually acknowledged Asclepius his better in medicine."

Phantastes clapped the book closed with a resounding noise. It shook Kay from a reverie, and she was for a moment conscious only of a face—the face of Rex, the porter from the Pitt, contorted in surprise and wonder—beyond the terrace window. She thought he, too, must have been listening to the story, and she struggled to recall its details; but her mind felt dull, and it was only with great effort that she summoned the image of Asclepius, standing among snakes, raising the body of Pelops from his bed to life again. The image, like the slow ooze of molasses sliding from a turned spoon, could not be rushed, and by the time she had conjured it, Rex was gone.

"It was also said, long after," Phantastes added, turning at last to Kay, "that Asclepius was finally destroyed by Zeus, who was enraged by his hubris and his skill in the lives and deaths of mortals. But in fact the great healer left Greece to join us in Bithynia, and he was one of the greatest imaginers among us. For integration—healing—and imagining go hand in hand; one cannot close a wound without the idea of a healthy body. And it is in the fate of Tantalus that perhaps even a child may glimpse the mystery of integration and its special power.

Tantalus was ordered by the gods to sacrifice his only son, who was his pride, his all in all, the only joy he had in his life; he was also punished brutally for his obedience, and some say he is being punished still. But Tantalus's cruel piety gave us also Asclepius: so the snake gives fatal venom, but also rebirth; and so too the imaginer conjures merely dreams, but those dreams—those stories—can show us a kind of higher truth."

"Will is always saying that," said Kay. Phantastes raised his eyebrows. "That stories are usually the best answers. Better than facts."

"Sometimes," agreed Phantastes, "they are. There are some—like Ghast—who have called us only forgers of lies. And to one way of thinking, that's just what we are. There was one piece of Pelops's body that Asclepius could not heal because it had been eaten by a dog—the shoulder. He made him a new one out of ivory. But this was a fitting loss, because it is always the dog, the unbeliever, who cannot be restored by our imaginings, who is leaden and impervious to the healing of the imagination."

"So lies—I mean stories—are good only for people who believe them?" Kay was struggling to hold so many things in her head at once.

"A story can work magic for the one who both believes it, and does not; for the one who knows it is true in a way greater than facts. If we are to recover your father, we will need an imagining of this kind—a great new vision; one that can inspire even a man who has lost everything, who has lost himself, with new hope, new purpose, new belief. New *self.* That is why Will has brought you here to me. Together we can find a story, a vision, that will help to recover your father. But before I can create that imagining, *if* I can, I need to know the point from which to work—the raw materials, if you will. I can imagine anything, of course, but in order to make an imagining that will mean something to your father, something that will resonate especially and perfectly with him, I will need—"

"A clue," said Kay.

Phantastes smiled. "Exactly."

"And so your friend, the little bald person—"

"Eumnestes."

"He is looking for this thing so that you can imagine a new story for my father?"

"Eumnestes reads the chronicles and histories, the stories, the epics and romances of earlier times. He knows all that has ever been done, and all that *might* have been done, and all that ought to have been done—that, or he knows where to find it. Eumnestes knows all the stories. In one of those stories I hope we can find the right idea. And with the right idea, an imaginer can produce such a vision that your father will not only rouse himself from his stupor, but sing and dance, too. We will find your father, and we will wake him."

"You won't find anything about him in your books," said Kay. "You'll find lots of things, but nothing that will speak to *him*. If you want to speak to *him*, you need *me*."

"Perhaps," he said softly. "Perhaps you are right."

And then, suddenly, the wraith looked down and scooped up some of the dried leaves, cupping them in two hands for Kay to see. "You know what these are."

"From the tree downstairs? But there are so many—"

"Hush," warned the old wraith. "None of them know about the tree or the temple. I haven't told anyone, so you and I are the only ones in the world. Ghast is a serious antagonist. If I can turn his acolytes to my service, perhaps he can do the same to me."

"But the tree is so small, and there are hundreds of leaves here."

"I gathered these leaves ten thousand years ago," said the

old wraith, almost laughing with a melancholy sigh as he let them fall back to the table. "When that trunk you saw was no jagged skeletal husk but a huge pillar of wood, and the leaves fell by the cartload every autumn. You had to be quick, of course, because the priests didn't take kindly to anyone stealing into the temple or pilfering bits of their tree; but I came away with stuffed pockets most of the time."

"Why did you gather them? What are they for? Cooking?"

"Yes, you might say that, yes. We treat it like an herb, and steep it in hot water. But it is not for nourishment. Come, I will show you."

Phantastes took Kay's suddenly tiny hand and drew her out into the hallway, then out through an open door on to a stone terrace—and for the first time since arriving in Alexandria, Kay felt the full force of the sun. Immediately she noticed that it was directly overhead rather than off to one side, or even long on the horizon. This sun simply beat down on the scalp, like a continuous falling of heated hammers. Underground, in the temple, the light had seemed gentle, nurturing; here by contrast it felt like an open and boring eye, seeing into both of them with an arid look. Everything around them glared with the light and heat of it: the stone balustrade of the terrace, where she set her hands as she looked down over the rooftops to the sea; the pebbles and sandy grit under her feet; even the water of the large circular fountain in which, to her initial surprise as her eyes adjusted to the light, Will was sitting—with his clothes on.

He looked sleepy—at least his eyelids were heavy and drooping, if not completely closed—and there were beads of sweat sitting proud on his forehead. The water poured out of one side of the fountain, and he sat in the pool up to his knees with his legs crossed before him. His hands hovered over the water, palms open and fingers extended, and seemed to be describing a slow, circular motion across the surface. At first Kay thought he was plotting, but this was something slightly different. And then his hands began to move in other ways, shaping through the air as if he were working with a soft stone or wax and forming, or deforming, the cut of a statue; but still his eyes never stirred, and the lids lay draped across them almost bashfully. His hands moved quickly before his body, now scooping up water from the pool and letting it pour very deliberately through the space before him; now pushing with great force down on some invisible shape being molded, stamped and pressed.

Eumnestes padded onto the terrace in his cotton slippers.

He moved with silence and intent directly to Will's side and, leaning over the wall of the fountain, whispered a few words into his ear. Phantastes let out a low whistle as Eumnestes stood back, nodded, then disappeared again into the house.

Looking around, Kay realized that several other people were also scrutinizing Will. Flip sat upright and poised on a low chair about three meters away, marking him closely and occasionally moving his own hands—involuntarily, she was sure—in the air at his side. To his right, a little closer to her, Rex leaned against the balustrade, almost perched on its top. Heavier than the two wraiths, and old, he gripped the stone behind him with hands that were gnarled and slightly empurpled. Kay tried to catch his eye, but he was watching Will intently and never looked her way, not even when she drew in closer to the little group and sat down on a low stone bench.

To Flip's other side, and on the far side of the fountain, someone else was squatting just over the edge of the pool. It was another wraith, a woman, with dark and glossy hair, almost purple in the sun, brushed back in tresses over her shoulders. Kay couldn't see her face well, but could anyway discern that she, too, had at least one eye on Will; and while Kay peered round the fountain's stem to get a full view of her face, she saw her do something very curious. She slowly reached into her pocket and drew out a dark black stone—no, perhaps a marble, for it was smooth, and gleamed like glass—but not glass, because she squeezed it easily, and it rained a kind of juice into the pool below before she rolled it between her fingers, and dropped it. Her actions were tiny and painfully slow, as if, with everyone's eyes on Will, she was anxious to avoid observation. She squeezed and dropped another, then another; and as Kay craned her neck to peer round the fountain, the wraith caught her eye and froze—and broke into a wide smile.

But it was at that second that Will's arms suddenly came to an abrupt halt in the air, his head lifted in a straight and decisive jerk, his eyelids shot up, and he stared straight at Kay. He said only two words, with perfect clarity and intensity, and then fainted, falling to his right into the pool. As he fell, everyone on the terrace scrambled to his side, except Kay; she sat there feeling nothing at all, the words reverberating in her head, the chilling, direct stare burning with a dark blaze into her memory.

"Andrea Lessing."

No. Not again.

She felt nothing—just a gaping, empty coldness.

Not here. Not again.

Everything seemed to move very slowly, soundlessly, and as if it were at a great distance: the hands pulling Will out of the water; a swarm of unfamiliar wraiths suddenly scaling the terrace from every direction; the body of Eumnestes falling from the second-story window and crashing, mangled, onto the stone before her feet; the cold, cold blade of the knife that, in the middle of that long moment, slid into the soft flesh of her right shoulder. Over the rooftops beyond the terrace, past the swaying tops of two glossy palms, Kay saw birds circling—circling, circling, but not landing—as she fell forward.

It had taken all the skill of forty of the greatest of the left-wraiths. They had plotted for weeks on Ghast's orders, composing the plan that would destroy his enemies once and for all. It had been a mighty effort; but then, it was the nature of stories, and of the feeble-minded wraiths who still told them, to make the simple look very difficult. From this vantage—that of the present—he considered the problems trivial, and the recent chain of events more or less inevitable. The once-great First Wraith could be relied upon for his incompetence. Having failed everyone around him again and again, he had made failure a kind of habit. He would fall easily into any trap laid for him if the bait were some promise of redemption. His companion Philip was of a subtler temper, but in that subtlety lay his vulnerability: believing himself to be too wise to be duped, he was after a manner duped by his own wisdom. The girl did not bear pondering: give her the slightest nudge, and she would move at a constant speed in whatever direction you chose, until you chose to alter or stop her course. She was so much water; one did but channel her. Ghast frowned. His enemies had proved weaker than he deserved.

Soon his runner would reach the barge with news of his agents' success in Alexandria. Already he had received his first report. Naturally his enemies had fallen like flies into the honey pot, exactly where Ghast had dropped them. With no friends left in the mountain, they sought out—and so betrayed—their last ally. It would be sweet to learn of the old imaginer's death; he had compassed it so often in his imagination he half thought he had become half an imaginer himself.

Now, having played his enemies, he would play his friends. Perhaps that would be more satisfying. In time to come, friend and foe alike would call him master.

"What is it?" he all but spat at his servant, who presumed to interrupt his reverie. The obsequious wraith winced to be acknowledged.

The barge was making slow passage through a wide, mostly rocky mountain valley. It was late in the afternoon. To the right Ghast noticed two of the large vultures that bred in the area, circling low as if about to land on the rough weeds and low shrubs covering the valley floor. He watched them thrust forward and extend their claws as they dropped to the ground. Their wing feathers stood out black against the gray light. Still his minion did not answer.

"I will tell you," he said, "what you cannot yourself contrive to say. You come to relay to me the news that the Builder, the man More, has been shaken off and left to beg for food in some ditch or alley at the end of the earth."

"Yes," said the terrified eyes of a lesser right-wraith.

"But you have worse news for me, too, and you fear to give it." He paused and stared hard into the quivering pupils of his victim. They contracted to terrified pinpricks. "The runner who came to you passed on this report and vanished, staking not his but your head on his message. And the message is that the little girl, More's daughter, the worthless one, has escaped with her friends. That's it, isn't it?"

The wraith nodded in a way that seemed to offer his head upon an imagined block. But Ghast had no more use for it than an overfed cat for a scrawny mouse. He did not even feel the urge to toy with him.

The barge floated untroubled down this quiet, broad valley. Soon they would put ashore for the night at one of the prepared landings. The girl had escaped by his design, but he would dissemble that; if his enemies were determined to be so hapless, he would have to help them to put up a fight—for only a fight, or the appearance of one, would suit his ends now. Meanwhile he must rouse himself to the performance of a purple fury. Soon the time of ruses would be over.

He longed for the ease of the vulture that never killed for itself.

11

First Wraith

For what seemed like years Kay lay with her face just beneath the surface of the cold water in the pool on Phantastes's terrace. Beside her lay Will, his eyes turned toward her, unblinking—but not dead, for he smiled from time to time, and his mouth seemed to move in a way that might, out of the water, have been speech. The whole time she lay in the sun-slicing pool, Kay longed to understand these frustrated words, to hear what it was that Will was trying to tell her with his untiring gaze and his kind, slow, exaggerated smiles; but no sound came, and every time she opened her own mouth, the salty water flooded in, thick and viscous, like blood.

Later, with faint surprise, she began to be aware that the world outside the pool was moving, and as time went by, she could see it with ever greater clarity. She struggled to lift her head to find out what was going on, but always the exertion brought back the taste of that salt water, and still she could not find her arms or legs, with which she might have braced or pushed herself. Soon she began to hear what seemed to be words, only just beyond her hearing, as if spoken through a thick towel. In time, this drone resolved, and words themselves gradually emerged, then snatches of story, then longer pieces—pieces of knights, and priests, and bankers, and voyages, and precious stones, and unscalable cliffs, of courageous attempts and pitiable losses. Hour after hour she lay in the pool, watching passively as the blurred world above the water shifted by, struggling to hold on to the sense of the slurred words swirling around her ears and keep the taste of the salt at bay.

It never occurred to her to wonder whether, or how, she was breathing. Her breath had poured out of her entirely, and in her lungs and stomach, there was only a desperate need to resist the water that engulfed her. But despite her resolve, she felt that she was failing, that it was seeping in at the cracks between her lips and at the corners of her mouth, that the pressure was massing at her nose and, when her eyes were open, upon her eyes. Slowly, drop by drop, the pool's thick water forced its inevitable way into her mouth and down her burning throat. With every drop the pain became more severe and she grew more desperate. But in time—how much she never really knew—it became obvious that the water was slowly draining away, becoming air. And as it drained into air, the sound of the voices around her changed from their droning to a more usual tone, and it was clear that the thick drops seeping down her throat were in fact air, and that what was forcing its way between her lips and pressing at her nostrils was not choking gulps of water, but essential, rhythmic gasps for breath.

Often, when she opened her eyes, staring sideways over the bleary pillow toward the window opposite her bed—for she was not, as she had thought, on Phantastes's terrace, but in a brightly curtained room—she found Will seated beside her. He spun yarns and told tall tales, stringing out long and engrossing stories with which to pass her time, and his, as she struggled back toward consciousness. Sometimes Kay followed them, but mostly the words seemed to float or hover just beyond her reach, like bright butterflies too light and quick, too mobile for her to grasp. She took in words by the hundred, by the thousand; but while she knew they were in sentences, and the sentences knitted up into actions, and the actions into stories, nonetheless they seemed to slip through her fingers and to settle around her—ungraspable—like so many flakes of ash.

Once when she woke, Will was gone. Kay stared at the window for a while, until the bright square of light had burned so fully into her field of vision that she could see nothing but her own blindness. Then there was a motion, and someone sat beside her—not Will, she knew—and began to tell her something very important. The words were urgent, though his tone was quiet. She squinted at his outline, and at the words, trying to make them out, but for a long time nothing would focus. He was speaking about Eloise. He was speaking about her father.

Whoever it was, he was telling her everything.

Kay knew that to any observer she must look entirely still, quiet, paralyzed; but within, in the silent fastness of her mind, she felt frantic. Her thoughts raced in place as she tried to gather up the words and speeches, the details, to hold on to them, to store them, to put one next to another, to make them stick. Every time she tried, like water from her hands, like gossamer in the wind, they drained and fluttered, slipped, shifted and sped away. She knew that these were words she needed, that they were secrets, truths, revelations, and the keys to going home. Inwardly she sobbed and screamed as she tried, and tried, and tried—and failed—to make sense of the things he was saying.

All the while she lay still, staring, her eyes slowly resolving the face before her.

At last, the speech ended, and he was quiet. The words lay in drifts around her, discrete and innumerable, like sand. Kay felt the impossibility of understanding them: Who can count the grains of sand? How can they be handled? How ordered?

And then her vision sharpened, and she knew the face before her. It was Rex, the old wraith that she, her mother and Ell had met that night at the Pitt. On Christmas Eve. The one that Phantastes had said was one of his. The one who had held Ell on his knee, who had said that something beautiful often happens just before—

"Do you understand, child, what I am telling you?" His face was kind, earnest.

Kay shook her head, a little, against the pillow. She hadn't understood a thing—only words that she seemed still to be juggling, shuffling from hand to hand, trying not to drop them.

He placed his tough, gnarled hand very lightly on her cheek, and smiled.

"That's okay. I'll come back. For now, I can't be seen here, even by the others—it's too dangerous."

There was a noise from outside the room—the sound of a door opening, or closing. Rex pushed himself to his feet, crossed the little room and climbed through the window onto a roof below. And then he was gone. In the bright air he left behind him, Kay could see the harbor with its little boats, and a long and narrow causeway stretching like a ribbon into the sea, and ending in a tiny island.

A few minutes later, Will sat again—as usual—by Kay's bedside. When he saw that she was crying, he seemed at first to think it was the pain.

"We're safe now, Kay," he said. "You had a concussion, and a very shallow wound to your shoulder. It's healing. It will hurt less every day."

Kay couldn't find her voice, but she managed to shake her head—very slowly, very weakly. *No, it's not that. That's not what it is.*

"We gave you some herbs to help you sleep. You'll be very groggy for a little while longer, but it should be starting to lift already. Soon you'll feel just fine."

Will. Listen to my eyes.

"Do you want me to tell you a story?" Will asked.

Kay tried to shake her head again.

"Do you want to know what's going on?"

She tried with every muscle in her body to push herself up, to speak. *Ell. Dad. How long?* Her eyes shouted at Will to hear her. Something in the rigidity of her exertion must have done the trick.

"Seven nights," he said. "Seven nights, Kay." Her body collapsed back into the bed. *Seven nights left.* From a great distance she thought she could feel Will squeezing her arm.

"It must have been Ghast. We're not sure how he found Phantastes, the house, the library." He stopped for a while and turned to look at the ceiling. Then he began again, not looking back at her. She saw that the room they were in had plain white walls and a low ceiling. The window still stood open where Rex had slipped away, and it was very light. "After Flip and I lost you in the tunnels, we went up a rear chute into the house—it's the way we always go, to avoid being seen on the street. We're always worried about wispers in Alexandria. For good reason, apparently. We saw Phantastes, he told us to start working on the integration, and—you can guess the rest. I don't know much about what happened once I was in the fountain. After you sit in a pool steeped with leaves, your mind tends to go blank a little—and you probably saw more of me and everything else than I did. But I think Rex was there, and of course Flip. And Katalepsis was there. Kat's a plotter, one of the few we've always been able to trust. She used to fly with Flip.

"According to Flip, that's when everything went wrong. There must have been at least four of them—assassins—because someone pushed Eumnestes from the top floor of the library at about the same time as two of them came out onto the terrace. One of them put the knife in your back." Kay tensed to hear out loud what she had assumed already. "It's going to be all right, Kay. It turned out to be a lot less serious than we'd feared. And Phantastes knows a lot of people in Alexandria, and we got you away quickly enough to make sure you were properly looked after. Flip was hurt a little, too, in the leg. But he's recovering well." Will looked straight at her and smiled.

"We gave you henbane, and poppy—for the pain, and to keep you asleep for a little while—till we were sure you hadn't snapped your neck, or that the knife . . ." He trailed off. "Anyway, you're fine. The two together put a person into a kind of coma. I guess you have been having some hallucinations"—Kay tried to nod, but only her thoughts moved—"and you'll be unable to move for a little while longer. And you'll have forgotten a few things. But don't worry. You'll be up and on your feet soon." He smiled again. Kay could tell that he was trying too hard.

Her head was pounding. There were thoughts squirming in her head, like bugs under a stone—but the stone was so very heavy, so painful. She willed it to move; even the willing was exhausting.

"We left Alexandria the next night. Phantastes insisted. He said it was too dangerous to stay. Kat said she'd help us. She went on ahead, here, and found this place, like a safehouse where we could stay out of sight, out of harm's way. Phantastes hired a ferry for us to follow. We've been holed up here in Naxos. It's a little island, not far from Greece, quiet, hidden. Beautiful. There's a myth about it, if you're interested—" Kay tried to glare at Will with her eyes, and he noticed. "Right, no stories. I forgot. Well, this is a nice house, just on the square—you'll like it. The streets outside are all cobbled." He stopped, and Kay listened to her own slow, quiet breathing for a long minute. "Don't worry: we left Alexandria in the middle of the night, and no one could have followed us. We're staying here long enough to get you fit again, while Phantastes tries to figure out what happened and then make new plans for the integration. Now that you're awake, it won't be more than a few hours—" Will looked at her again. "We'll find him, Kay. We'll find both of them."

She lay there with questions pounding in her head. She wanted to hear about Ell. Did they know where she was? How would they find her? What could she *possibly tell her mother*, assuming, of course, they ever made it home again? How could she explain that she had lost her little sister? Kay was so tired she could hardly think, so paralyzed she couldn't even tremble; but she sobbed all the same, huge tears, that, even if they could not run down her cheeks, still ripped through her silent body. Above all, she wanted to tell Will that Rex had come to her, had spoken strange words to her, that he had climbed from the window the moment Will had come into the house.

But I can't move my face.

Will came and went many times over what seemed like a few, long hours. Kay slept in bursts: sometimes she lay for interminably long periods on the side to which Will had gently rolled her, facing either the window across the floor or, in the other direction, the white, immediate surface of the wall running up behind the bed. From beyond the window, she thought she could occasionally hear a snatch of something that might have been children crying. On the second day, only a few minutes after dawn had soaked into the room with its pale, gauze touch, and feeling for the first time very alert, she realized that the crying children were seagulls.

Will strode into the room and smiled broadly. He had evidently been waiting for her to wake. "Kay, I think you're well enough to sit up. And if that goes well, we want to take you outside."

Kay clenched her teeth and put out her arms, feeling the tightness draw back between her shoulder blades and a dull pain in her upper back. She found she could move, but only with great effort. The words in her mouth moved so slowly she felt she had to lay them, like eggs. "Will," she said quietly, "where is Ell?"

"We're working on that," he answered as he righted her, gradually shifting the weight onto her waist and reaching for some pillows to put behind her back. Her head swam. "We've tried to imagine a way out of this mess, and it didn't work. We're going to give plotting another go."

"I . . . don't . . ." she said slowly. The words came out in a near whisper.

"Right," he said, taking a seat by the bed. "You understand

plotting well enough, I take it—how it's done?" Kay nodded, a little, less than she meant to. "Most wraiths can do a little plotting, though some are better than others. There have been a few that had no knack for it at all—like Phantastes. He was never a plotter." Will looked right into Kay's eyes and said in a whisper, "He doesn't even have a *board*." Kay nodded—after her conversation with Phantastes in the Temple of Osiris, this didn't surprise her at all. "A wraith who can't plot can't plot for one reason, and one reason only. A wraith who can't plot is an imaginer."

"And Phantastes is . . . the last of the great imaginers . . . or very nearly," Kay said quietly, each word a battle. She sank back onto the pillow Will had placed behind her.

Will looked at her with a sharp, curious intensity. "He *is* the last. Did he tell you about the others?"

Kay shook her head, once.

Though he sat silently enough, Will had suddenly become very agitated, and the silence was as loud as—louder than—the low tolling that still sounded in her ears.

"As far back as anyone can remember, there were always three great imaginers, since there were imaginers at all: Asclepius, Phantastes and the Siege Vacant. Asclepius was destroyed—his hubris—we do not speak of it, and a lesser right-wraith takes his place on ceremonial occasions—but the Siege Vacant—it has gone by other names—"

"Phantastes told me . . . Asclepius . . . but not . . . the other, the Siege—"

"That's because it pains him to speak of it. Unlike the other two imaginers, the Siege Vacant is an open position, filled by one of the lesser right-wraiths when the need arises, but never when the Weave is summoned; there the seat is always left unoccupied. And this is why. I told you before that the knights are a thousand and one in number, but this isn't strictly true. It is said that the first of the imaginers left the Honorable Society long ago, and hasn't been seen since—the first of the imaginers, gone before my time, and no one knows where or why. Phantastes leads the imaginers now, but the empty chair—it has, ever after, been known as the Siege Vacant—an office never quite filled, because Phantastes believes, somewhere in his heart, that she will return."

Kay pushed herself up painfully on one elbow. "She?"

"She is said to have been the greatest of the imaginers," Will replied. "It is even said that she built the great loom. She was called Scheherazade." He vented a long sigh.

Scheherazade, Mother of Stories, called the Breaker of Kings, the Freedom of Kingdoms, Scheherazade of the thousand tales, the healer, the seducer, the beguiler. Kay's body shook once, violently, and she sank back on to her pillow, looking up at the empty ceiling.

"Well," Will went on, "I suppose Phantastes told you about the tree of Byblos and the Temple of Osiris. It was thousands of years ago, but he still remembers the old places with a kind of reverence, and it was inevitable that he would go back there. You heard me mention the leaves before?" Kay nodded gingerly. "That tree is—was—very important to the imaginers because chewing its leaves puts you in a state—of creativity, or epiphany—and the imaginers used to gather them fallen, and sometimes steal in to the tree to pick the more potent fresh ones, when it still grew in the Temple of Osiris. One of the three imaginers was pretty much always in Alexandria for that reason. I don't know if Phantastes explained to you exactly what it is imaginers mostly do, but they often use the leaves for their imaginings, and it is a great good fortune that Phantastes had gathered so very many of them in the years before the temple was destroyed and the tree hacked down—he dried them, and has been using them ever since."

"He showed me," Kay said. *And I have touched the new, green leaves springing from the body of the god. And I have held the shuttle to my lips, and I have sung of love in the sacred Temple of Osiris.* It all seemed so magical, so far away. Now she lay in the bed, marooned in the middle of some unknown ocean, no less brittle and dead than that old, fire-scarred stump.

"We should have foreseen, when the armies burned the temple and replaced it with churches to their blind gods, what it would mean for the imaginers. Without the tree, Phantastes had to ration the leaves. Without new leaves, Phantastes and the others would hardly dare imagine; and this weakened them, and their standing with the wraiths. It was during this most difficult time that Ghast, who has always hated imagining, and all the imaginers, first began to attract notice. The lesser plotters started to adhere to him and his ideas, and it wasn't long before his star, as it rose, began to eclipse the imaginers completely. Ghast is a plotter—but, to be honest, he is a poor one, and he might never have succeeded in seizing power in our great assembly, the Weave, except for one thing. Now, Kay, listen closely. That thing is the House of Razzio in Rome."

As he spoke, Will adjusted Kay's pillows and straightened

the light sheets in which she was partly wrapped, but now he came to a full stop, in action and word. He looked troubled.

The throbbing in her head had subsided, and Kay was feeling stronger, increasingly alert and steady. Thoughts that had been circling over her head for hours, for a day, seemed to be condensing, to be falling into place. They were appearing bright, shining, and discrete, like dew on blades of grass in the still of the morning.

"But how could anyone—have preferred *Ghast* to *Phantastes*? Phantastes—he's so *kind*."

"Necessity," said Will simply, his eyebrows arching as he dropped his head, defeated. "Razzio is the greatest of all the plotters—he is to the plotting wraiths what Phantastes is to the imaginers: their spiritual head, if you like. In Rome he has the greatest board in the world—two halls cannot hold it, nor a kingdom purchase the tenth part of its beautiful craftsmanship. It is laid in a floor all studded with gold- and silverwork, and above it twists an arbor of branches and vines, with clusters of huge fruit hanging hidden behind the evergreen foliage. Beneath your feet the lines run for what seems like forever. And he doesn't use stones. Two hundred wraiths—he calls them the causes—walk the boards where he calls them to and fro, and he constantly moves among them, trying out patterns, thinking about relationships, working through stories, and coming to know the beginnings and the ends of things. In all this he is served by two other wraiths—deputies, if you like, or lieutenants. By tradition we call them the modes, and they are in a way the soul of Razzio's house. In the huge and sprawling palace that surrounds the board lives Oidos, moving in the silent rooms of the place of pure knowing; to her, Razzio resorts to learn the meaning of what he sees plotted on the board. At the center of the board, upon a raised platform roofed with stone, the other of the two modes, Ontos, dances in silent gyrations. His platform is known as the place of pure being, and while Razzio is on the board, Ontos never leaves it. Working with Oidos and with Ontos, Razzio has become the master of all there is to know about how causes create effects, and effects in turn become new causes. He can show you the million threads that ravel in and unravel out of every event. Everything in the House of the Two Modes comes from something else, and goes to something else. Everything makes sense. It is only there that my hands can truly be still.

"Razzio is a great genius. He has only one flaw. He is very vain. He made up his mind before all time that his way of understanding the world was the right one, and he cannot stand even to share the same room as Phantastes, or for that matter any of the imaginers. For his part, Phantastes will not tolerate Razzio any more than Razzio will acknowledge Phantastes; and so, when Ghast came to Razzio with a plan that, he said, would drive the great imaginers out of Bithynia for good, of course Razzio jumped at the idea. From his house in Rome he sent an army of his acolytes—all greater left-wraiths—to join with Ghast's left-wraiths. Together the two factions began to dominate and determine all the councils held in our ancient hall."

"The Weave," Kay offered.

"Yes. When the wraiths still gathered in Bithynia, once a year—in midwinter, on the twelve days—the twelve knights of Bithynia would return from their journeys, wherever in all the corners and edges of the earth they were, to celebrate the festival of renewal. From Alexandria the three imaginers; from Rome Razzio and the two modes, Oidos and Ontos, the eldest of the plotters; from Lebanon in the east the three youngest of the left-wraiths; from Atlas in the west the three youngest of the right-wraiths. Over the twelve days the twelve knights would mark the festival with storytelling competitions, poetry competitions, song, dance and of course the feasts—the likes of which I think the world does not elsewhere know: for sumptuousness, for high revelry, for state and for goodness. Oh, Kay, the Shuttle Hall—"

Kay's gaze had fallen upon the red hem of the blanket gathered in her lap. Now she lifted her eyes to regard Will as his voice faltered, and saw very briefly the tears already collecting on either side of his chin. Every movement that each of them made, because effortful, because delicate, seemed an oration.

I can't bear your tears.

After a few moments and a long breath, he began again. "In the great hall, the Shuttle Hall, where the tiny diamonds in the ceiling, like stars, constellate and shine all night long in the middle of winter, and the mosaics on the floor sweep in foamy tides across shoals of pebbled thought, there did we feast, sing, tread the paces of the ancient meters, create and re-create stories that, had they been told in words out of some forgotten language, still you would have wept for joy, and fear, and joy and fear, only to hear the sound of them. And every wraith in the world came there once a year, and the twelve knights did all this."

Kay found that her hands were gripping the blanket so tightly that her fingers had turned white.

"On the last of the twelve days of the festival, when each of the twelve knights had held court for one day, the general assembly and synod of the Honorable Society took place. In the stalls to one side of the hall the plotters took their seats and, opposite them, the imaginers. First, before anything else could happen, the great horn was sounded, the peal of the Primary Fury—a blast like chaos, like all the clamors of the world gathered into one, shocking the very air and ripping through ears and heart, a cacophony to clear every thought, every fantasy from the minds of its hearers. Then, as the horn's furious note faded, all eyes marked the procession of the twelve knights as they passed down the length of the hall in silence, each wearing the insignia of his or her order, each carrying one of the twelve staves of the Honorable Society—iron rods crowned by a writhing snake and a plotting stone. One by one the knights stowed their staves in the great wheel at the center of the hall, where the light from the windows dazzles the floor with blue like sapphire; one by one the knights took to their thrones. Then the First Wraith entered, and walked the length of the hall. From the twelve knights he received the shuttle—fashioned from the most luminous, pearlescent stone, whorled and flexed, dimpled and notched to take the pirn—the bobbin or spool—and with it the thread wherewith the weft is worked against the warp, and the web woven. The First Wraith blew upon the shuttle, a call harmonious to answer the great horn, music after fury, choosing a note that would set the tone for the story and the debate to come—love or war, tragedy or quest."

Kay remembered the resonance of that lustrous horn, its furled and compact mystery, its gleaming inward. Even now, with the thought of it, some nerve within her, as if struck by a velvet hammer, vibrated, and her core tingled.

"In that sound, as if in an embrace, as if enclosed and fortified in completeness, the mystery would truly begin. To you, Kay, a wraith must seem a strange sort of thing. We are here and not here, large and real and substantial, but fleeting, evanescent. We come and go like lights in the night. To you perhaps we are like angels, participating in your moment-to-moment, but somehow eternal. You cannot understand. But we are not so strange, if you think about it. What is love? Can you see it? What is justice, or truth? Can you touch them? Can you pour them into a bowl or throw them at the wall? But you know these things *are*. So I am, so Flip is. And so, to us, the Bride is—as ravishing as an epiphany, so beautiful in our thought and trust that she is Beauty itself, a form fleeting and fugitive; but as real, as eternal, as important as the greatest and most certain truths. Most people would do anything for love, for truth, for beauty. These things are absolute and the greatest goods. In just this way wraiths and phantasms live and die by the Bride, for in her, as she touches us and informs us, as she makes us who we are, we all participate in her as the flower does in scent, as the sun does in brightness, as the sky shares in blue and trees in green. In her we are joined, we are wedded, to our own being—more, we are wed to being itself, united with all that is in the world. A poet once said that no man is an island. The Bride is the reason why. Through loving her, through believing in her, we are all brought together into one society, into one truth, into one beauty.

"At that sound of the shuttle, if the heart of a wraith is clean, the Bride enters. I cannot describe it to you except to say it is like a star at dawn, and like the dawn, too, something you become aware has been there all along, something that heralds, something that floods. Her presence steals over you like the blue light falling from the windows of the Shuttle Hall, and gathers, as if in a stone, as if in a luminous sapphire that you could hold in the palm of your hand, so real is her presence, so complete her assurance. The moment in that sound has a name: we call it the Bridestone—for what reason no one knows, or it has been long forgotten, but it lasts forever, though it is over in the blink of an eye, though it flies through your heart like a swallow through the length of the hall, in at one window, across a single instant a-flutter and a-dart, and then out the opposite end. And yet an instant is enough, for there, in the presence of the Bride, time sways in its deep and the least ripple of its tide is an eternity.

"In the synods of old, the First Wraith blew upon the shuttle and then sat at the loom, and he wove as the wraiths rose to speak, each one a thread around him, and the day's assembly with all its voices moved the First Wraith's hands, and the tapestry he wove there was the great record and judgment of the assembly, in which, should you read it carefully, you would see every moment of that day and its concerns, alive and speaking in the cloth by color, texture, pattern, contrast, subject. As you might imagine, we have thousands of them—I think you have seen some of them in the tapestry room in the mountains?"

Kay nodded. She heard the whisper of a light footfall then and, following the sound with her eye, noticed Flip leaning in the doorway. He smiled faintly, meeting her glance for a moment before looking back at Will who, oblivious to his audience and engrossed, went on.

"The First Wraith was, you might say, the soul of the convocation and its mouth. Through him everything passed and was resolved; through him and through the motion of the shuttle in the threads of the loom. But the voices were those of all the wraiths, speaking if not in harmony then in symphony. We clashed, I don't deny it; but our wars and campaigns found their way into the images we made, and from them flowed back into the stories we told, and spread abroad into the world for everyone to see, and to know, and to tell, to handle. But Ghast—what he did—it is almost unspeakable.

"Because in that year, when Razzio sent his plotters from the house in Rome and they plotted in the mountains the overthrow of the old order, the festival was held as always, and we feasted and reveled for the twelve days and nights, and the Weave assembled, as ever, and the shuttle was placed in the hand of the First Wraith, and he sat at the loom—and—and there was utter, unspeakable silence."

Here Flip drew in a sharp breath, and Will spun round violently on his chair, throwing his hands before his face before he realized, just as quickly, who it was. He turned back wearily, breaking.

"A few wraiths spoke—they tried to start the story, the

debate, to find the theme, to gather up the threads—but as in weaving you cannot work a warp without a weft, one thread against another, so in debate, in song, no voice can speak alone, no song take flight without its undersong. A great debate, like great music, is the work not of a few but of many voices. The First Wraith, seated at the loom, tried to weave to this broken noise, and the loom lurched now and again, the shuttle clacking within it; but at the end of the day we were left with only some straggly and disconnected patches of fabric. There was no image, no border, no *pattern*. It was as if some huge weight which we thought stable and permanent had suddenly shifted, and because of its weight had crashed and broken all around us. We have never held a Weave since, and the festivals slip away, year after year, into memory. I have not heard such a song these two or three hundred years.

"But it didn't end there. It had hardly begun. For by the end of that day Ghast had mounted the pedestal, seized the shuttle from the very hand of the First Wraith and had it cast into the sea. The loom was dismantled and, I was told, fed to the fire. The halls that year were shut, and boarded up, and at Ghast's command the Honorable Society retreated into the mountains, the barbarians at our heels. And we left the mulberry orchards, and we left the plotting gardens with their winding streams, and we left our great library with half our books, and so many other things, all abandoned, all deserted in fear and without hope, without pattern, all haphazard. And the festivals were discontinued, and the twelve knights were sent to the twelve compass points of the earth, Kay."

"And Ghast set the First Wraith to work doing common removals," added Flip softly, from the door.

Kay's eyes shot up, in pain, to Will's crumpled form where he slumped on the chair, his long legs drawn up to his chin, wrapped in his desperate arms. "You," she breathed.

"At your service," he answered. But he didn't look up.

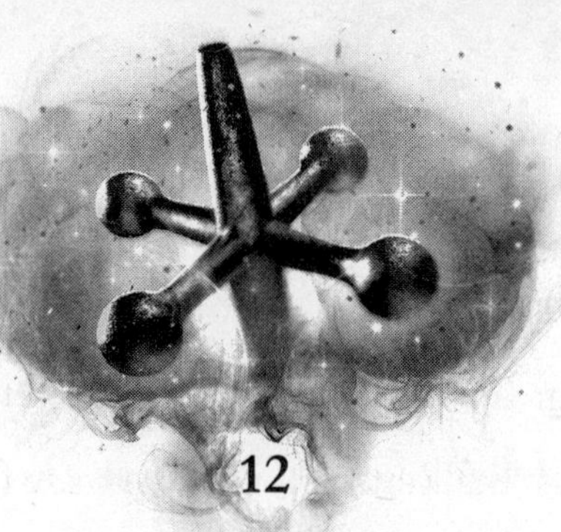

12

BETRAYAL

With only a few words, everything had changed. Kay had lain in the bed for how long she wasn't certain—for days, surely—but suddenly felt she had only just arrived, had only just been born, had only just met these fallen heroes, these crumpled titans that sat and stood before her. She squeezed her eyes shut, trying to take it in, trying to understand why this revelation had sent an electric current tingling through her spine and along her limbs, to burst from her fingers in sparks like surprise.

Will was nodding his whole body slowly, without looking at her. It was as if he were rocking himself to sleep, and when he carried on talking, his voice was a nightmare lullaby. "At first Ghast had me imprisoned for misleading the Honorable

Society—for making false images. It was clear what his real target was; clear enough. Everyone knew. The old synthesis, Kay, was between the imaginers and the plotters. Always, since time was, the great rift has yawned between these two ways—the warp against the weft—those who create from nothing and those who believe only in causation. The plotters cannot accept that the imaginers conceive, and the imaginers cannot suffer the sterile mechanics of the plotters. To the plotters, the imaginers are charlatans; to the imaginers, the plotters are machines. This has always been the great divide. All our tapestries represent this conflict in one way or another, because as First Wraith, all my purpose was to synthesize and bind these two functions. Ghast wanted to end it; to use his alliance with Razzio to give the plotters the upper hand. He called it 'progress.' He called it 'a new era of efficiency.' But, Kay, he had many of the imaginers dispersed."

Kay's eye settled on the leather satchel Phantastes had given her, in which she was sure the shuttle still lay, waiting for the touch of its master. It was only at the foot of the bed—she could reach it, give it to Will and change everything, give him a salve for his grief. But something in her didn't dare. Perhaps it was because Phantastes had told her to wait, had warned her, and she trusted him. But there was something deeper, too—it wouldn't be right to put so beautiful a thing into the hands of a wraith who was still so . . . so broken.

All the while he spoke, Will stared over his knees at his hands; they lay there, drained of color, the knuckles like white peaks in a rough landscape of time and suffering. Kay stared at them, too, and thought of the mountains from which they had flown without Ell, not knowing where she was or how to reach her, how to recover her, how to take her home again. Kay tried to picture in her mind how Ell would be feeling: the emptiness, the fear, but also the wonder. Sometimes Ell loved to be lost—at the beach it was sometimes hours before she turned up after lying in the shade of some gorse bushes at the head of a low cliff, playing with the thistle tops. All that time she would watch walkers passing and ships sailing on the sea, and never cry or worry. Perhaps, Kay thought, this time it would be the same. *Maybe she is somewhere calm and quiet. Maybe they have been good to her.* The alternative wasn't . . . It wasn't possible to think about it.

She was still staring at Will's hands when Phantastes barged into the room, all strides and grand gestures.

"Boys, Katalepsis is back from the piers. She thinks she's

seen some wispers shadowing down by the harbor. She doesn't think they've found us yet, but they're definitely in the city. We don't have long. We may have to move on, possibly tonight. Next ferry at noon, then another at sundown."

The other two wraiths bristled.

"But that's not everything," continued Phantastes. He stood in the doorway, his eyes a piercing cerulean against the tanned and weathered skin of his face. "The market was heaving with people, so I can't be sure. But I thought I saw Rex."

"Here?" Will swiveled abruptly and sprang to his full height. His eyes instinctively sought the view out the window. "Wait. How could they know we are here? How could they be in Naxos at all? No one could have followed us on that night crossing. And no one could have seen us come in through that storm." He looked jerkily around at all of them in turn. "No. This is too close, too fast. They found us here like they found us in Alexandria. This isn't plotting. There's something else going on."

"Spying?" Phantastes said.

"Will," Kay said, trying to cut in—but her voice was too weak.

"It's a leak," said Will.

"But who?" asked Flip, stepping fully into the now crowded small room and pulling the door shut behind him as he did so. He and Phantastes sat at the end of Kay's bed.

"Will," tried Kay again.

"We need clues," Will said. "We need to remember exactly what happened in Alexandria."

"Will, we've been over this," Flip said. "We've been over and over it. There's no new information."

"*Will*," said Kay again, summoning all the power of her diaphragm and chest. She threw his name out like a javelin. It hit him like a straw—but it hit him. He looked at her, his nervous plotting energy in suspension.

"He was here," Kay said. "Rex. Yesterday." They all looked at her with curiosity and confusion. "In this room. Here. He talked to me."

"You were hallucinating," said Will. "He wouldn't have come here. We think—" He paused. "Kay, this is hard, but—"

"We think he might have betrayed us to Ghast," said Phantastes flatly. "We can't understand why, at all—Rex is the oldest wraith in the mountain, and no friend to the new ways—but he disappeared during the attack, and we haven't seen him since." Phantastes put his hands on his knees, as if he were straining to get up, but he wasn't. His arms sagged. "It's the only explanation."

"No," said Kay. "It's not."

"Kay, it is," said Will, "hard as it feels to accept it."

"But if he's here, now, in Naxos, today"—Phantastes had turned with renewed appeal to the other two wraiths—"we may be in very serious danger. And unless we move fast, we can give up all hope of going back."

"Going back where?" interrupted Kay, again. Her stomach had turned, but this time it wasn't the henbane or the poppy.

"To Bithynia, of course!" cried Phantastes, with impatience. "So, boys, again, once more, think back. If they didn't track you through the air and they couldn't have plotted your movement before you left, then how did they find us in Alexandria?"

"I don't know. I didn't *see* anything unusual," Will muttered. "No suspicious faces. No patterns in the street. No following noises. And there was no one at the house but Flip, Rex, Kat, me—and Kay, of course, and Eumnestes."

"*Will.* Will *nobody* listen to me?" Kay pushed herself up on her elbow. "Katalepsis—Kat—she was the one with the beautiful hair?"

Will nodded.

"There's too much," Kay said. "In my head. It's all a fog. Wait. I need quiet. Just for a minute."

The wraiths waited. As the seconds pulsed by in her temples, Kay could feel their agitation, their worry—for her, for their home, for their safety. They were deeply absorbed in their thoughts, she knew—running over every detail in their memories, trying to remember. Will's and Flip's hands were twitching as they picked through threads of consequence that led to the assassins, to Eumnestes's fall, to the cool steel in Kay's back. She could almost see the webs and branches opening up in the air before her as they thought, and she longed to pick through them with her fingers. *Perhaps I am developing this plotting skill after all.* In her own mind she saw the terrace, saw the wraiths clustered around it, the sun on their heads, saw Will in the fountain, his robe soaked as it floated around him, his eyes empty, and something—

Will broke in on her thoughts.

"No, it's just the same. Everything is the same. Up until the fountain I saw and heard nothing that made me in the least suspicious; and after that it was a sealed house—nobody went in or out. Are you sure, Flip," he said, turning from the window, "that you haven't forgotten something?"

Flip shook his head. He looked uncertain, Kay thought, but still he shook his head.

His eyes empty, and something—

Will turned to Kay. "And you didn't see anything, Kay? Nothing at the beach, nothing on the streets? Nothing in the sewers? Nothing in the house? Nothing on another terrace maybe? Nobody watching?"

"No."

"It's so incredibly frustrating," Will said. "To be under the leaf at all is bad enough—but that integration was so hard, so painful. I wasn't aware of anything at all except the pain. And then their timing: to come in like that, just at the end, when our concentration was most absorbed, when I was most engrossed and groggy—it was uncanny. It was like they were waiting for a cue or something."

Something was tapping Kay on the shoulder. She could feel some detail, some half-remembered observation, stirring in her memory. It was something important, she thought, but the poppy was in her way.

But if it were something important, wouldn't I remember it?

Then it struck her. *At last. Kat.*

Kay leaped into the conversation so vigorously that she felt her back twinge.

"Where do you get the leaves for the integration? When do you add them to the fountain?" she asked.

"You know where we get them," Phantastes said. "I showed you—on the table. That was my entire store, all that I had left. We add a few to the fountain an hour or two before the integration so that the leaves can leach into the water. I readied the fountain as soon as we saw the plane."

Kay blew out a long breath. She spoke with gathering pace. Her energy was returning, stretching into her limbs and fingers. "Then what did I see Kat slipping into the water while Will was . . . integrating? Is that what you were doing?" She looked from one to the other of them. "When I first came onto the terrace, I saw her take something from her pocket, and as she dropped it in the pool, she looked right at me. She smiled at me. It was small, dark, glassy—maybe like a marble, or a—I don't know. I couldn't see over the edge of the fountain well enough, so I don't know what happened to it, but it looked heavy when she dropped it. It certainly wasn't a leaf."

Phantastes looked at Will. Will looked up. "Belladonna," he said.

"The obvious poison," agreed Phantastes. He slumped now, but said—to Kay, though he might have been talking to himself, "The symptoms of belladonna poisoning are almost the same as the effects of the leaves—dilation of the pupils in the eyes, twitching of the hands and feet, lethargy and sleepiness, loss of speech—only it is fatal. We would never have suspected anything. Oh, it all fits: Will complained afterward—while you were sick, Kay—of strange side effects from the integration. The lethargy, the loss of his voice, the aches in his joints. But more importantly we know that Katalepsis is highly skilled at administering it; unfortunately she has done it for Ghast in the past. We just never thought she would do it to *us*."

Phantastes spun in front of the door, wedging his arms into the frame, and fixed a look of contempt on Flip, sitting at the foot of Kay's bed. Flip simply dropped his head into his hands and said nothing. But it was Will who spoke—spoke, or groaned with words.

"Flip. I don't understand." Will held out his hands, together. "Kat was your call, your friend. You've known all along that she was playing us, haven't you." It was a statement, not a question. "How could you bring her here, let her do that?" He stopped. Kay thought he was plotting for a moment, but then realized that his hands weren't thinking—they were shaking. Will's body was sobbing, though his face looked completely clear, empty. "How much did you know, Flip? The assassins? The wispers? The little girl? Flip, what did you know? Why have you done this to us?" Will stared, but he didn't seem angry. Full of fear, Kay watched his stoniness and drew back gingerly into the corner of her bed, taking up her knees under the blanket. "Flip, we could have *died*."

When Flip raised his head, Kay half expected to see his face covered in tears; but while he seemed rigid, there was no grief in him. He held his face level with Will's and spoke only to him.

"Of course I didn't know what she would do. Of course I didn't know what Ghast would do. I had his word . . ." There he stumbled, and his eyelids dropped momentarily. "I thought I had his word."

"But whose word do *we* have, Philip?" Phantastes was angry, almost shouting, boxing at the air with his teeth. "Whose word for us? What truth is in you? How can we call you friend now?"

"You can't, obviously," said Flip—evenly, quietly. "I know that. I knew that. Although you should, now above all. Although I have never been a better friend to you, Will, than I have been in this." His eyes met Will's, and the two friends regarded each other impassively. "You can't know this now, but you will see it later. What I have done—everything—I have done it to protect you. Remember this, Will," he went on, still staring directly and unblinkingly at him, "remember that I told you here, now, that you would come to know not just what I have done, but how I have done it. Remember."

Flip sat rigidly, unmoving. He might have been a stone or a tree trunk. Not even an eye twitched as the two wraiths continued to stare at each other, their hands stilled, their breathing imperceptible, their arms now stiff and straight at their sides. Their friendship was passing between them, Kay thought, but she hardly cared. *Traitor.*

Phantastes took two quick steps, threw back his head, and with a snap of his neck spat at Flip's unflinching brow. "If you have any friendship left in you, you will leave this place and us, and you will never return to the mountains, to Bithynia, to the company of other wraiths. If you have any friendship in you, you will not go to Ghast with this, or with any of our plans. Now get out."

Flip stood up painfully, as if his limbs ached, as if he were an old man. He drew out the sleeves of his gown and smoothed his front—but he never wiped his face. "As for you, Phantastes," he said slowly, "I have never given you cause to hate me, and I give you no cause now. I will wear this contempt, but not for my own shame. I will wear it for yours." And with a resolute and even step he let himself out of the white, still room. The sound of his footsteps quieted and fell away.

Flip's departure had left an unbridgeable silence, and sadness, in the room. Kay's eyes settled on the window, where it still stood open a few feet from her bed. But only for a moment.

She sat up like a shot, before she was even sure what she would say. She fumbled.

Rex.

"Will. Rex. He's here. He *is* here. But the reason he's hiding—"

Will turned wearily to her, and all the rigidity and strength of his confrontation with Flip was gone. His mouth labored words. "What? Kay?"

She found her thread. "He's not hiding from us. He's hiding from *her.*"

Will looked at her, stunned.

"He sat at my bedside, in that same chair where you're sitting now." Kay felt her blood rising now, as it hadn't in days. Her muscles tensed, and she shivered with heat. A torrent of words stacked in her mind; her mouth was too small a vent to release them. "He told me something, something important, but I was too delirious to take it in. He talked about Eloise, about my father." There was enough blood stirring in Kay's veins that she blushed, a little. "I think he talked about *me.* He told me secrets, the answers to everything. I had the distinct feeling that he was giving me the *key* to it all. And I couldn't move, couldn't understand the words. When you came into the house, he climbed out of the window, over there—" Kay leaned forward, almost easily, and raised her arm like a sign of power, to point out the window toward the little harbor that she could now see, its stunningly clear blue water like a shell of beauty laid at the feet of the mountains to every side. "He climbed out of the window, and disappeared. All I remember is that he said, when he left—he told me that it was too dangerous *for you,* to know that he was here. He isn't your enemy. He's trying to protect us all. From Kat."

"Kat wouldn't dare—"

"To hurt Rex? Are you sure?" Kay swung her legs to the floor, and took a deep breath. Her lungs ached with disuse. "Where is she now?"

"At the harbor—just beyond the market—"

"If Rex is there, too, then he is in danger."

"She's right," said Phantastes—but all three of them were already scrambling to the window. Kay winced and caught her breath, hard, as she staggered to the wall and braced herself against the frame. Through the pain she saw the low roofs beyond their little house, then trees, then, beyond that, illuminated in bright winter sunshine, the central square of the city, with its flagstone pavements and low, run-down buildings. She could see almost the whole of the market, just as Phantastes had described it earlier, and as it came further into focus and her eyes made the adjustment from fever and sleep, she saw people. At first she thought they were dancing, because they all seemed to be skipping to the center of the square—twenty or thirty people, from all directions.

"By the muses," Phantastes whispered, sheer as a knife.

All those people had formed a kind of ring, and within it Kay could just make out, over the top of someone's head, the dark, luxurious sweep of Kat's hair, gleaming in the bright morning sunlight. There was too much commotion to see quite what was happening, but from the surge and hush of the people, it couldn't be good.

Then she saw him: his silver hair, his solid, heavy frame,

the strength and wisdom of his ancient face, even at this distance—like a light standing in the harbor, on a dark night—piercing through the crowds, sweeping over the rooftops.

Rex.

Will was already gathering the last of his few things. He lifted Kay's coat from the back of a chair, and draped it across her shoulders.

"Whatever Rex said to you, whether you can remember it or not, it makes you very vulnerable," he said. Phantastes was still staring out the window. "When she's finished with Rex—"

"I'm next," said Kay flatly.

"We all are," said Will. "Phantastes, you said the next ferry was at—"

"Noon," answered the old wraith. He peered around the edge of the window to take the time from a clock mounted in the city's market. "Ten minutes."

"We're going to be on that ferry," said Will. "Can you walk, Kay?"

She nodded.

"Can you run?"

She shook her head. "Maybe," she added.

"That's the spirit."

Will held her arm with such strength and courtesy as they went down the house stairs that he might as well have been carrying her. Out through the tight front hallway, they filed into a little alleyway that led to the main square. Ahead they could see the crowd still pushing toward the shore, still engrossed in the spectacle of Kat and Rex. They hurried into the square and away from the commotion, huddling against the walls as they skirted a long path toward the piers.

The last twenty meters, Kay saw, would be open ground—out onto the flat cobbles between the market stalls and the concrete promenade from which two short wooden piers extended into the bay, out into the full view of the crowd and the two wraiths at its center. From the knot of people came calls and shouts, taunts and whistles, but it was obvious that no one dared approach Rex and Kat. Kay could only imagine what held the people's gaze, their attention, their fascination—she could only imagine it, and yet she didn't dare to think. Instead she tried to concentrate on her feet, keeping them steady, keeping her ankles firm as she took step after step, stumbling to keep pace with Will and Phantastes.

When they reached the pier, Phantastes stopped to haggle with a ticket seller. Will stood with his back to the harbor, shielding her from the commotion beyond, but it was no use: Kay couldn't help but see beyond him the narrow causeway stretching out into the bay, at the end of which a little island lay like a jewel of green and stone in the wind-fresh blue. On it stood the ruins of the ancient temple: a single stone plinth atop two columns, stark against the sky as a gallows. The crowd still lingered at the harbor's shore, but Rex and Kat, fighting hand to hand, had drifted on by quick sallies and parries down the narrow strip of land, moving ever further and further toward the island. Kay watched them go, willing Rex to defend himself, willing Flip—*where are you?*—to appear, to break through the mob, to rush to Rex's defense, to save him. But he didn't. He didn't, and he didn't, and the two stepped, blow by swift blow, out of reach.

Although she was facing them, her back to the sea, Kat hadn't seen them. Her eyes were on her hands, on her enemy. Up and to the left, the ferry's engines rumbled into life. Will wrapped his arm around Kay and shepherded her over the gangplank onto the boat deck. Phantastes followed, and they found a berth toward the front, where they would be sheltered from the wind and spray during the four-hour crossing. Kay settled against the high back of the bench, and tried to gather her thoughts. She knew it was urgent that she remember.

He said something. Eloise. He said Eloise was my sister. He said she was my sister and I must go to her.

Kay was digging the fingernails of her right hand, hard, into the back of her left. She went over and over the words she could remember, but couldn't make them add up. *Sister. My primary duty to my sister. She is the third from the left. Sister. Go to her.* Nothing made sense.

A ripple and murmur of agitation ran through the people sitting on the deck around her. Kay looked up. They were all staring to starboard, craning their heads to see over the wales of the boat, craning their heads to get a glimpse of Kat and Rex, still fighting on the causeway. Will and Phantastes, among them, had climbed onto the seat beside her, and were staring intently across the water. Silently, hardly more than slipping into place as a leaf might fall to the earth, Kay joined them.

It was unbearable. Kat and Rex had reached the island. Even from this distance, it was obvious what was happening. The two combatants held one another close, grappling for purchase, strength against strength. This was the endgame.

These were the final moves. Around Kay the tension rose in the onlookers even as their murmuring died to nothing. The rumble of the ferry's engines, ominous, like drums, foretold the fall to come. Kay held her breath. She counted the seconds as Kat and Rex, embracing for the last time, held one another like lovers.

And then he fell. He fell as a tree falls, silently and with moment, crashing not through the forest but through the dense growth of watchers, through the great air of his age, falling not in pieces but wholly, crushingly, deadly, to lie upon the earth forever, and not to stir. His fall as he fell they all felt was final, the last staggering collapse of something truly mighty.

"So passes from this world the second form of the Primary Fury," said Phantastes, quietly. "Who now will blow the blast to summon the Weave?"

Kay's thoughts exploded. In Phantastes's words, like a key turned in a lock, she suddenly saw the importance of all that Rex had said to her. *Not the third from the left. He said he had left the third form. Not my primary duty. My duty is to the Primary Fury. He said I should go to her, to his sister. To his sister, who would lead me to the third form.*

"No," Kay whispered. *That wasn't all. He said more. Rex.*

As the others watched, mesmerized, stricken, while Kat set off at a dead run down the causeway, back toward the shore, Kay slipped from Will's side and threaded the gathered passengers as she made her way to the gangplank. The engines were roaring, and the boys ran along the pier, uncoiling ropes from the posts that held them and tossing the heavy loops onto the deck. Kay came to the ferry's gangplank and, finding the barrier down, climbed lightly over it, so that her feet perched on the very edge of the ferry's deck. The boat was pulling away from the pier, lumbering into motion as the water churned in deep swirls around it. Summoning all her strength, she leaped for the pier—

And landed, already running, her gait matching stride with Kat's as the wraith tore down the causeway toward the parting crowd. Kay felt herself flying, her thoughts calling, *No, no, no,* with every extension of her legs, with every heave of breath in her lungs, with every swing of her arms from their sockets. She gained the market and took the near corner onto the causeway as Kat—who never saw her, racing through the wide passage of onlookers who parted to allow her through, then closed after her—passed into the market and disappeared. Kay sprinted across the causeway, aware to her left of the ferry drawing up to speed as it pushed across the harbor to the breakwater, Will and Phantastes still standing like sentries, tall and anguished, on its foredeck. She didn't dare turn toward them; she didn't dare break her own stride, for fear that her courage would fail her, but on, on across the causeway without consideration of the consequence she ran, and the wind dropped off the mountain, through the town, and bore her along.

Rex, what did you say? What was the key to it all? What was it that was so dear to Kat, to Ghast, that you could not be suffered to tell me in plain sight?

At the end of the causeway Kay traced the tracks that, scuffling and grappling arm against arm, Kat and Rex had made in the grit of the island's little slope. She climbed, her thighs aching, at a spring, bounding from ledge to ledge. Her eyes were fixed on Rex's trunk where he lay a little curled, facing toward the sea. She examined his body for the last rise and fall, the least twitch that might show he was still clinging to life.

As she approached him, dropping to a staggering, halting walk, not only her courage but her strength drained out of her. Kay panted, choked on the air, panted again, almost retching against the pain that seared her lungs, her sides, her legs, her shoulders. She was sure he was dead. That he would answer no more questions. That he held no secrets, still, for her.

Five or six steps from his side, Kay stood doubled over, her head swimming, when Rex groaned and kicked out his left foot behind him, twitching in the dust.

"Rex, Rex," she called, hurrying to huddle at his face, "it's me, it's Kay. Rex."

He opened an eye. Blood soaked his stomach.

"Katharine," he said. His mouth moved as if to smile, and was caught in a terrifying rictus. Then it relaxed. His eye, wet with sorrow, seemed to sparkle.

"You must go to my sister," he rasped, scraping the words out across his own mortality like metal bars across stone. "Go to my sister, and she will take you to the third form of—the third—"

"Of the Primary Fury," Kay finished for him. He smiled again, this time as fully and warmly as he had on that first night, at the Pitt, when he had held Eloise in his lap and soothed her anguished tears.

"In Rome," he whispered, "in the House of Razzio. You will find her there." Again Rex's leg twitched, and Kay saw him slipping away, his body reducing with each labored breath.

"You must get there before—six nights more. That is the only way you can save your—beautiful—sister."

Kay nodded, vigorously, strowing tears from her cheeks across the barren, rocky ground of the island. She longed for this kind old man to sit up, now, and take her on his knee as he had done her sister, to soothe her troubled heart, to wipe away her tears. Instead, crouching quickly to the ground and cradling his head in her lap, she tightened her eyes and, breathing deeply, steeled her heart and made a vow.

I will go to Rome for you. I don't know how, but somehow. I will go to Rome to your sister. I will go to Rome for Eloise.

"You know," Rex said, dropping to a whisper, "I was wrong. I was wrong when I said that something beautiful sometimes happens before a calamity." On the last word he choked, and coughed, and the coughing in deep shoveling spasms graveled through his dying body in a contortion of such clotted, irredeemable pain that Kay had to look away, and all her two fists were not enough to wipe the streaming tears from her cheeks.

"I was wrong," he said again, at last, as the coughing subsided. "Wrong." He paused, breathing shallowly. "Sometimes something beautiful, something impossibly beautiful, happens right—*after* a calamity. Trust me," he said, and with great effort he drew up his hand to touch hers. She gripped it.

"I will," she promised him. "I promise that I will."

Kay was looking at his eyes as they opened. Into her mind, abruptly, came the feeling that she had sensed earlier, that Rex's gaze was like the beam of a harbor light, like the sweeping, penetrating beam of a beacon that warded treacherous coasts on fatal nights. And she knew, with that light in her eyes, that the promise she had made him was right and total, and that it would lead her to the end of her story.

"I promise," she repeated.

Kay slid her hand back beneath his head, and looked out to the harbor, where the ferry was passing through the breakwater. Will and Phantastes still stood on the starboard deck, their heads and shoulders proud of the high railings, their robes flapping in the wind behind them, watching, never turning for a moment, never breaking for anything their vigil for their friend, and for the lost little girl they were leaving behind.

"Katharine," said Rex, in a voice almost as still and indistinct as the wind coming to them across the water, and she knew that these were his last words. "There is something else. I saw—you—" His breath failed him, and his whole body shuddered. "Will—" he said.

"He's gone," Kay answered, her words clipping Rex's with all the urgency of the flecked breaths spitting from his pale, pale lips.

"Will—will—save us—"

Not now, he won't. They were gone, the ferry now on the open water and picking up speed, but Kay could feel the two wraiths' eyes still on them. Unrelinquishing.

And then the shuddering ended.

Kay held his head between her hands for a long time. At length she laid it on the stone, and kissed it, once. Then she sat on the hill that overlooked the harbor, and as the winter afternoon descended into a cold evening, watched the ferry dwindle against the horizon.

Six nights. How will anyone save us now?